PRAISE FOR JENNIFER JAYNES

". . . intricately plotted . . . The action builds to a jaw-dropping conclusion."

—*Publishers Weekly* on *The Stranger Inside*

"Talented Jennifer Jaynes turns up the intensity with her first standalone thriller: *The Stranger Inside*, an edge-of-your-seat crime thriller solidifying her place alongside the best of female crime writers out today!"

—JDCMustReadBooks

"Jennifer Jaynes writes a smart and twisty thriller that's guaranteed to keep you reading well past bedtime . . . I am anxiously awaiting the next book."

—Gregg Olsen, *Wall Street Journal* bestselling author of *A Wicked Snow* (on *Don't Say a Word*)

"Jennifer Jaynes serves up pulse-pounding suspense with a large helping of heart . . . She's an author to be reckoned with."

—J. Carson Black, *New York Times* bestselling author of *Darkness on the Edge of Town*

"Jaynes dazzles with shocking twists and turns that will keep you riveted to the very last page."

—Lisa Regan, award-winning author of *Finding Claire Fletcher*

"Jennifer Jaynes has quickly become one of my favorite writers. Her stories are deep, dark, and twisted . . . I can never turn the pages fast enough."

—Winter Renshaw, *Wall Street Journal* bestselling author of *Royal*

"The ending was mind blowing. There were so many shocking twists and turns one right after another, I was truly left speechless when I finished this one . . . Can't wait to read more from this amazing author!"

—*The Princess of Everything* on *The Stranger Inside*

DISTURBED

OTHER TITLES BY JENNIFER JAYNES

The Stranger Inside

Strangers Series

Never Smile at Strangers
Ugly Young Thing
Don't Say a Word

DISTURBED

JENNIFER JAYNES

 THOMAS & MERCER

This is a work of fiction. Names, characters, organizations, places, events, and incidents are either products of the author's imagination or are used fictitiously. Any resemblance to actual persons, living or dead, or actual events is purely coincidental.

Text copyright © 2017 by Jennifer Jaynes
All rights reserved.

No part of this book may be reproduced, or stored in a retrieval system, or transmitted in any form or by any means, electronic, mechanical, photocopying, recording, or otherwise, without express written permission of the publisher.

Published by Thomas & Mercer, Seattle

www.apub.com

Amazon, the Amazon logo, and Thomas & Mercer are trademarks of Amazon.com, Inc., or its affiliates.

ISBN-13: 9781542046381
ISBN-10: 1542046386

Cover design by Rex Bonomelli

Printed in the United States of America

For Christopher and Ryan.
You boys will always be my proudest achievements.

PROLOGUE

November 1, 2010
The morning after Halloween

IT WAS ALMOST 1:00 a.m. A living-room window was half-opened, and a thin, lemon-colored curtain billowed out as chilly morning air streamed into the small apartment. A slice of streetlight illuminated blood spatter on the cheap beige carpet and the motionless body of a teenage girl. Blonde and slender, she lay on her stomach, naked except for a pair of low-rise blue jeans. Detective Robert Lang stood in the doorway of the apartment and assessed the scene.

Blood stained the far wall of the living room, and a crooked scarlet trail led into a darkened hallway. The apartment smelled like stale smoke, spilled alcohol, and the metallic odor of blood. Lang also caught another scent he knew far too well.

Fear.

No matter who the victims were, no matter their gender, religion, social class, or circumstances, the bitter, acrid stink of their fear always smelled the same.

Lang had been intercepted in the parking lot of the apartment building by a concerned neighbor who'd reported the screams to the 911 dispatcher. The neighbor told him the occupants of the apartment were three young women who attended Springfield College. He said that several of the building's tenants were students, so random screaming and other loud noises were heard often—especially on nights like Halloween. But he said the screams he'd heard had been different.

As Lang's eyes locked again on the girl's body, his pulse pounded in his temples.

It never failed.

Even though he'd been working homicide for five years now, every new case felt like his first.

A voice called from the hallway that led to the bedrooms. "You got here quick."

It was a young officer named Brandon, the first responder on the scene.

"I was in the neighborhood," Lang said, his voice hoarse with sleep.

"I'm still sweeping," Brandon said.

Lang nodded. "I'll be careful."

Lang dug a pair of latex gloves and blue polyethylene bootees from his jacket pocket and slipped them on, then moved carefully to the body and knelt.

The victim was young, a year or two out of high school at most. Her head was turned to the side, and her milky-blue eyes were wide and staring. She had multiple stab wounds to her back and legs. Too many to count without a formal examination.

A couple of feet from her lay a white bath towel. An empty pizza box was splayed open on the coffee table, along with an empty whiskey bottle and a plastic two-liter bottle of Diet Coke.

"There's another body. First room on the left," Brandon said, pointing.

Lang stood and moved into the hallway. He stopped at the bedroom and peered in. Another girl. This one lay on top of her bed. Her sheets were twisted around her, and a pink comforter lay in a heap on the floor. A lamp next to her closet had been overturned, and blood was spattered across one of the walls.

He walked to the bed and squatted down to get a closer look. She looked about the same age as the first girl. Eighteen, maybe nineteen. Her face was a sickly white-gray, her mouth open as if frozen in midscream. Blood was matted in her stick-straight auburn hair, and it stained her T-shirt and jeans.

Sirens wailed in the distance as Lang got up to move to the other side of the bed.

Brandon yelled from across the hallway. "I've got something!"

Lang drew his weapon and moved carefully into the hallway, toward the sound of Brandon's voice. He found the officer standing in front of the bathroom doorway, his gun also drawn.

"Movement." He motioned with his chin. "Inside."

Lang nodded the go-ahead and pivoted to the left. Brandon struck the door with his foot, sending it flying open and banging against the wall on the other side.

Lang rushed inside to find a young woman cowering in the corner of the tub. She was curled tightly in the fetal position, shivering. The room was freezing. The odor of blood and the sickly-sweet scent of vomit hung in the air.

Lang looked up and saw the small window above her was wide-open, the wall leading up to it smeared with blood, as though she'd struggled to climb out.

His eyes flicked to a message scrawled on the bathroom mirror in what appeared to be red marker:

YOU MADE ME

Frowning, he went to the girl and kneeled next to the tub. Her clothes were drenched in blood. From the location of the bloodstains, he could see she had suffered multiple stab wounds, at least one of them deep in the side of her abdomen.

But she was still breathing.

Christ.

"Call for EMTs!" Lang barked.

She opened her eyes halfway and shielded her pale face with blood-covered hands. "Please . . . nnn . . . noo . . . ," she whispered, her voice thready. "Plee-aase."

"We're the police. It's okay. You're safe now."

Behind him, Brandon was making the call for an ambulance into his radio.

The tub's porcelain bottom beneath her was slick with blood.

Too much blood.

He scanned her wounds to see if any were more severe than the others.

The girl slowly spread apart her fingers, revealing glazed, bloodshot eyes. Her dark pupils were grossly enlarged. Her blue, chapped lips trembled. "Oh, my God. Ethan . . ."

Lang snatched a white towel from a bar next to the tub and began to apply pressure to the side of her abdomen. She winced at the touch, and the towel immediately turned a deep crimson.

"Ethan?" Lang asked softly. "Who is Ethan? Did he do this?"

From Brandon's radio behind him, Lang heard the dispatcher respond that medics were already on the scene.

"It hurts so . . . so . . . bad," she stammered, her voice barely a whisper.

He heard movement from the front of the apartment. More responders were filing in. Hopefully the paramedics. He could feel the warm blood pulsing through the towel onto his hand.

"It's okay, hon. It's going to be okay," he said, hoping he sounded reassuring.

Her teeth started to chatter.

He shouted over his shoulder: "I need medics, dammit! She's going into shock!"

Lang returned his attention to the girl. "Help's here now. You're going to be okay. Just hold on, hon." But even as he said the words, he doubted she would. It was clear to him that she was already dangerously close to death.

Her eyes fluttered, and her shivering intensified. The rest of the color drained from her skin.

"You've got this, hon. Hang on, okay? Help is almost here."

She stared at him for a moment as though she was maybe listening; then she moaned, and her eyes rolled into the back of her head.

CHAPTER 1

October 4, 2015
Four years and eleven months later . . .

TWENTY-THREE-YEAR-OLD CHELSEA DUTTON jerked upright in bed, adrenaline thundering through her veins. She fumbled in the darkness until her hand found the bedside lamp. She snapped it on, flooding her bedroom with warm light.

She blinked, and the reality of where she was slowly trickled into her consciousness. Blood still pounding in her ears, she fell back against her pillow and exhaled forcefully.

You're safe, she told herself, rubbing goose bumps from her upper arms, her fingertips stumbling a little on the raised ridges of her many scars.

You're safe and sane. No one's out to get you.

Not anymore.

The words had been her mantra for almost five years now. Since the Halloween night that her college roommates had been murdered and she'd been carved up and left for dead. Sometimes, though, she wondered if being dead would be easier.

She grabbed her iPhone to check the time: 3:00 a.m.

She'd been waking at 3:00 a.m. all month. A surefire formula for always being exhausted. In an effort to slow her heart, she focused on the weighted blankets piled over her body, enveloping her in a synthetic, makeshift womb. The extra-plump down pillow that rested beneath her head. The calming scent of lavender lingering in the air from the diffuser she kept on her bedside table.

A few of her creature comforts.

Comforts that she took great care to surround herself with. Comforts that proved life could actually be okay if she continued to try really hard.

You're in a good place now.

But even as she muttered the words in her head, she questioned herself. Because although things were getting better, she still believed she wouldn't be missing anything if she checked out for good. Since the murders, she'd been merely existing, not really living. Not only that, but in the attack four years ago, she'd suffered a severe concussion and had been diagnosed with psychogenic amnesia, which made life even more confusing and frightening.

Her doctors told her there were no guarantees whether she'd recover any of her lost memories, much less all of them. A few had come trickling back over the years, but nothing of real significance. Sometimes she'd get a flash of a memory here and there. Usually scents brought them forward. The smell of pizza reminded her of the night of the attacks. The sharp scent of Pine-Sol brought her back to living with one of her many foster families. The horrible stink of death reminded her of her biological father.

The flashes were like missing puzzle pieces, but they were brief and blurred—and there were still too many missing to form a decent picture.

Through both fragmented memories and the file she'd received from the Department of Children and Families after the attack, she knew that her biological parents had been dead since she was six years old. In their place was a long string of foster families whom she'd lived with until she turned eighteen and started college at Springfield.

Her cat, Harry, meowed, jerking her back to the present. "Good morning, sweet boy," she said, scratching him behind his ear. Then she sighed and slid out of bed. Knowing she would be unable to go back to sleep, she decided she might as well be productive.

Her eyes tearing up from exhaustion, she slipped on her running clothes, then cracked open a two-ounce energy shot and drank it. Finally, she grabbed the razor blade that she kept carefully wrapped in a square of cheesecloth and tucked it into her bra.

Harry meowed again, then stood and stretched his long, slender body. Standing in the middle of the bed, he eyed her, wanting to be fed.

"Not until six," Chelsea said, grabbing a small bottle of pepper spray and slipping it into the other cup of her bra. "You know the routine. Go to sleep. I'll be back soon." She grabbed her keys, the metal cool against her palm.

The city of Boston was still dark, hanging in that serene space between the bustle of late night and the promise of a new day. The crisp, early-morning air was chilly against her face as she started down the same route she ran every day—three blocks down Newbury, around the public gardens, back up Beacon Street to Mass Avenue, and then up Newbury to Dartmouth Street.

Exactly five miles.

Five miles unless she encountered anyone else on her path. When she did—which was rare this time of morning—she quickly detoured.

As she ran, she deconstructed the scents in the air: spicy wood smoke and vehicle exhaust. Chicory, espresso, and freshly baked bread and pastries. Even though she tried to concentrate only on the scents drifting through the air and the rhythmic sounds of her footfalls on the hard pavement, she could feel her memories from that horrific night creeping into the forefront of her mind. The night of the murders clung to her, no matter how determined she was to move on.

In the first years after the attacks, she'd found it shocking that the world was still spinning, the sun still shone, that people still laughed and went on with their lives despite what had happened that night. How life could just march forward, everyone completely unscathed, seemed almost obscene.

She could fully remember only the first couple of hours of the party before waking to find herself freezing and in excruciating pain in the bathtub. It had been Halloween night, and she and her two roommates, Christine and Amy, had skipped the normal Halloween parties to celebrate Amy's birthday. Chelsea had invited Ethan, a guy she'd gone on two dates with, and he had brought his roommate, Boyd.

Chelsea had been excited when Ethan showed an interest in her. Ethan came from a wealthy family and could have any girl he wanted at Springfield. Probably any girl he wanted—period. He was drop-dead gorgeous but also keenly aware of it. He had an air of privileged entitlement about him and a reputation as the type of guy who got around—a lot. Typically, those were qualities that would instantly turn her off, but he was also incredibly charming and funny. Besides, it wasn't like she expected anything serious to come of it.

But Ethan also liked to party. When he showed up at the apartment, he had whiskey and Ecstasy for everyone. Chelsea didn't like to drink and never did drugs. She didn't like the sensation of losing control. But Christine and Amy had quickly popped the pills and happily accepted the drinks Ethan passed out.

Ethan had teased Chelsea about not drinking, and she had eventually relented and drunk a glass of whiskey and Diet Coke. And before she was even done with her first glass, Ethan was beside her, handing her a second.

She remembered feeling as though she was a mere outsider as she sipped her drink and listened to Ethan, Boyd, and her roommates discuss the summer houses their families had up north while they became increasingly wasted. Halfway through her second drink, she'd been surprised when the room started to get blurry. She remembered Ethan's roommate, Boyd, saying he had to leave for work. Something about delivering pizzas and hating that he had to work the late shift. She recalled how Boyd's intense blue eyes had lingered on hers before he left the apartment.

After Boyd was gone, Christine and Amy began dancing in the middle of the living room, playfully grinding against each other, laughing and tossing their hair.

Amy recorded most of her college escapades and often uploaded the footage to her YouTube channel, where she already had more than six thousand subscribers and four million views. Her channel was something she'd taken very seriously—and one she made a good income from, at least for a college student.

Chelsea remembered hearing the spring squeak beneath the couch cushion as Ethan sat down. He leaned toward her and kissed her neck, his breath warm and smelling strongly of whiskey. Then he roughly slid a hand up her thigh, and she pushed it away. She was too dizzy, too queasy.

"What's wrong?" he asked.

"I . . . I feel really weird."

His eyes flashed. Then the couch squeaked again, and Ethan sauntered over to her roommates and began dancing between them. She still recalled the combination of scents in the living room that night: whiskey, cigarette smoke, and leftover pizza. The odors were powerful and made her feel even sicker.

She remembered the room tilting and noticing a little mouse—one that they'd been plotting to catch—skitter across the kitchen floor and pick up a fallen piece of pizza crust. That was her last memory before everything faded to black.

The next thing she remembered was a sudden burst of noise, the freezing cold, and white-hot pain knifing through her body. Then two men. One of them, Detective Lang, told her they were the police and that everything would be okay.

But he had lied.

Things had *not* been okay.

They hadn't been okay at all.

At the hospital, they had treated her for a punctured liver in addition to eleven other stab wounds and a severe concussion. They also replaced the four pints of blood she'd lost. Her doctors said she was very lucky to be alive. That someone had been watching over her.

Ethan had quickly become the key, and only, suspect in the murders. Among other evidence, they'd found his fingerprints on the knife block that was thought to have held the murder weapon. He'd also vanished that night, and no one had seen him since. Talk around campus had been that his rich parents had jetted him out of the country the morning after the slayings. But the theory had never been confirmed.

All these years, Chelsea had lived in a state of fear and paranoia, haunted by the thought of his possible return. She'd fled Springfield and moved ninety miles east to Boston after the murders, telling herself she was safer there.

There were so many lingering questions about that night.

Why had he spared her?

Had something scared him off?

And the most frightening question of them all:

Would he return to try to finish the job?

What exactly had she seen that night that was now locked up inside her brain, rattling around in her skull? She was pretty sure she didn't want to know.

The blast of a horn jerked her out of her thoughts. She leaped back onto the sidewalk just as a white box truck barreled past her. Trying to catch her breath, she looked around and realized she had been running on autopilot. She was now deep in the Warehouse District, where trucks were leaving for their morning deliveries.

Tiny spikes of fear rushed through her as she turned to retrace her steps. It took her a minute to get her bearings; then she sprinted in the direction of her apartment. She was usually hypervigilant when she was outside the safety of her apartment, so the thought that she had wandered unconsciously off her path terrified her. And the fact that she was so terrified made her angry. She was sick and tired of being frightened. She didn't want to play the victim anymore.

She wanted to be strong, not weak. Confident, not afraid all the time. She'd been told that healing from events as traumatic as what she'd been through would take time, but she was running low on patience.

The sky was gunmetal gray when she arrived back at her building. She placed her palms against the rough bricks, stretched, and forced herself into the right mind-set. To think about the day ahead of her.

Every day had its routines.

Routines kept her grounded and sane.

She leaned back against the apartment building. There still weren't many people out, but the headlights of occasional passing cars were beginning to break through the morning's stillness. She watched them pass, listening to distant voices being carried on the wind. People up above and down below, also getting ready for their days.

Then something caught her eye. A car parked on the other side of the street. Someone was sitting behind the wheel, partially concealed in the shadows. She watched for a moment. And then the headlights from the next oncoming vehicle splashed into the car and illuminated the driver's face.

A bolt of terror shot through her.

The man behind the wheel threw the car into gear and pulled out onto the street. Then, in a flash, he was gone. She'd only seen his face for a second, but that was long enough to recognize him.

Ethan.

CHAPTER 2

CHELSEA SAT ON the edge of her couch, blood thrumming at her temples, as she watched her friend Elizabeth walk to the French doors that led to the balcony. She pulled open the curtains, and morning light burst into the living room.

Elizabeth turned to face her. "Okay, so back up. You're saying he was sitting in a car? Across the street, with his headlights on?"

Chelsea nodded. "Yes."

"But it was still dark out, right?"

"Yes. But a car passed him, and the headlights lit up his face. I'm telling you. It was him."

Elizabeth walked to the recliner, her powder-blue orthotic nursing shoes squeaking against the Pergo floor. She sat down. "Look, I know you *believe* it was him. I do," she said, looking at Chelsea with clear but polite doubt in her green eyes.

I know you believe *it was him.*

She hated when Elizabeth said that, and she said it a lot. Unfortunately for Chelsea, though, Elizabeth was usually right.

Concern creased Elizabeth's face. "Did you have the nightmare again?"

Chelsea knew when she'd called Elizabeth and asked her to come over that she'd ask that question. Yes, she'd had the nightmare. But she had the nightmare *every* night. She'd never been exactly truthful about that with Elizabeth, though. She kept it a secret because she didn't want Elizabeth to worry about her any more than she already did.

"Chels, you see the pattern, right?" Elizabeth asked. "This happens almost every time. You have the nightmare, and then you *think* you see Ethan."

Chelsea shook her head. "No. This was different."

Elizabeth got up and paced the room, her arms folded over her chest. "Yeah. This time he was in a car. But it's happened in stores. You've seen him in crowds. At the airport. On buses. In coffee shops. On the T," she said, ticking off the city's subway system on her fingers and the other locations Chelsea thought she'd seen Ethan over the years. "And always when you're stressed out from that terrible nightmare of yours."

Okay, well, maybe that was true, but this time—

"Look," Elizabeth said. "I'm not fighting you. I'm on *your* side. But I honestly don't think it was him." Elizabeth leaned closer to her. "You've been through a lot, Chels. More than any human being should *ever* have to go through. But because of that, your mind tends to play tricks on you. Convincing ones. Take my word for it. Ethan's long gone. And he's not coming back."

Doubt started creeping in, like it always eventually did, and suddenly Chelsea found herself questioning whether she was positive it had been Ethan.

Chelsea's cheeks grew warm, and she peered down at her fingernails, which she'd gnawed into stubs. She shook her head. "God. I'm so sorry."

"For what?"

Her eyes teared up. "For letting my mind get the best of me. For freaking out all the time. Involving you in all my wild-goose chases and always being wrong about seeing him."

"Are you kidding me? You do know how much I enjoy being right, don't you?" Elizabeth joked. She knelt and stared into Chelsea's eyes. "And, girl, you're hardly a head case. You're a survivor. You're strong."

Chelsea watched Elizabeth's cheek jump a little, the way it always did when she told Chelsea she was strong, or anytime she *bent* the truth or told an outright lie. It was a tell Chelsea had learned years ago.

"And don't *ever* worry about involving me in any of your wild-goose chases. I want to help. Seriously. I'm here anytime you need me. I want you to know that."

Chelsea wrung her hands, then got up to feed Harry. She prepared his breakfast and freshened the water in his bowl, even though she knew he wouldn't come out until Elizabeth left. "I appreciate your help. I do," she told Elizabeth. "But I need to be stronger. To be able to do this on my own. I won't always be able to come to you for help."

"Why not? I'm not going anywhere. Seriously, you worry too much."

Elizabeth was right about that, too. She *did* worry too much, even though she tried not to.

Elizabeth stood up and went to the kitchen. "By the way, you need to stop running while it's still dark out. That's how you get yourself featured on the evening news."

That's all I need, Chelsea thought. She crawled back on the couch and pulled a chenille throw around her and watched Elizabeth move around the kitchen.

She couldn't be more grateful for Elizabeth. She was a loyal and steadfast friend. They complemented each other perfectly. Elizabeth had a burning need to take care of someone. And Chelsea had needed someone to take care of her.

She was the mirror opposite of Chelsea in every way. While Chelsea was brunette, petite, and quiet, Elizabeth was blonde, curvy, and outgoing. If she hadn't met Elizabeth, Chelsea was certain she wouldn't have survived the years that followed the murders.

They'd met nearly five years ago, in the Springfield psychiatric hospital where Chelsea had been held for three months after attempting suicide following the attacks. Elizabeth had been one of the nurses assigned to Chelsea's pod. Although Elizabeth was seven years Chelsea's senior, the two connected almost instantly and stayed in contact after Chelsea's discharge. Then when Elizabeth transferred to a hospital in Boston, Chelsea eventually tagged along.

"You should start getting ready for the farmers' market. Things get picked over quickly, and besides, the cute guys shop early," Elizabeth said with a wink.

Chelsea sank even deeper into the couch. "I'm not so sure I want to go out again today."

Elizabeth strutted into the living room and reached out her hand. "You are going. You need to get out of your head, and that's not going to happen if you're just lying around here."

Elizabeth was right again. They always hit up the farmers' market on Saturday mornings. No need to break the routine and end up feeling out of sorts the rest of the day.

Chelsea let Elizabeth pull her to her feet. "Okay. Fine. But at least let me take a quick shower. I'm pretty gross."

"Expecting to meet someone?"

Chelsea laughed. She had vowed to never get close to a man again, and Elizabeth knew it. She rolled her eyes. "Yeah, right. Over my dead body."

CHAPTER 3

CHELSEA PULLED HER blue fall sweater tight against her body, buried her face in the pink chenille scarf looped around her neck, and tried her best to seem okay. Plastering a smile on her face, she tried to focus on the beautiful displays at the farmers' market.

The sun was working overtime to suppress the chill in the October air. Bostonians were outside in droves, soaking up every ounce of warmth before the long winter forced everyone inside. Chelsea tried to distract herself from her anxiety by concentrating on the rich colors of pumpkins, gourds, and winter squash, pints of homemade soup, and canned jams and jellies.

She fingered the razor blade in her coat pocket, soothed by its mere presence. The blade was her security blanket—in case she ever found herself slipping mentally again and needed an escape. She'd vowed years ago that she would never suffer through the misery of a debilitating depression again or another attack. She'd much rather be dead.

She scanned the crowd, looking for Ethan. Her mind flashed back to the news coverage of the murders, and the photos of Ethan that the media had constantly splashed across the television screen. His high school graduation photo. He'd looked so innocent in it with his short, blond hair and whiskey-colored eyes.

Stop thinking about him.

Elizabeth had been right.

I didn't see him this morning.

I've never seen him.

"Hey," Elizabeth said, snapping her back into the present. Her eyes serious, she leaned in and whispered, "Your mind was playing tricks on you."

Chelsea laughed. "You're in my head again."

"What can I say? I have mystical powers." She smiled so widely her molars showed. "And you aren't very good at hiding what you're thinking." She nudged Chelsea's shoulder. "It feels great out today, doesn't it? I love this crisp air." Elizabeth tilted her face to the sun and inhaled deeply.

Chelsea couldn't care less about the weather. She'd much rather be in her apartment with all her comforts. Away from the crowds, from the possibility of Ethan watching her without her knowledge. "Yeah, I guess it does," she agreed.

Chelsea noticed a little boy grinning at her. His mother looked at her oddly, then quickly grasped the child's hand and walked off.

It was just one more reason Chelsea didn't like being around a lot of people. Ever since the murders, she'd noticed people often looked at her strangely.

Was it because they were repulsed by the raised three-inch slash mark that still extended from her nose to her left ear? After all, it wasn't every day that you saw someone sporting such a big scar, especially a woman. Or was it because people recognized her face from all the ghoulish national-media coverage? She didn't know.

Elizabeth grabbed her arm. "Come on. Let's go find some cider doughnuts."

Chelsea started to follow Elizabeth's lead, but when they turned around, she stopped cold, her breath leaving her with an audible whoosh.

A familiar man was standing no more than ten yards in front of her, checking out a stand that sold frosted cookies and other freshly baked pastries.

"Oh, my God," she whispered.

"What?" Elizabeth asked, frowning. She looked in the direction Chelsea was staring. "Chelsea, that's not Ethan. That guy doesn't even look like—"

Chelsea shook her head. "No. It's not Ethan. It's Boyd."

"Who?"

"Ethan's roommate. Boyd. Boyd Lawson."

His dark hair was a little shorter now, but otherwise he didn't look much different. She was positive it was him.

"Elizabeth, he was there. The night I was attacked. He's the guy who left early to deliver pizzas. Remember me telling you about him?"

Elizabeth's frown deepened. "Yeah, I think so."

"I want to go talk to him."

Elizabeth arched a slender eyebrow. "You think that's a good idea? Revisiting old wounds? I thought you wanted to start over? With a blank slate?"

She did want a blank slate. But she also felt an urge to talk with him. A strong one.

"I do, it's just . . ."

Chelsea's gaze swung back to Boyd, who was now walking away from them. He'd be lost in the crowd within seconds. She'd have to hurry if she didn't want to lose him.

"C'mon. Cider doughnuts are calling our name," Elizabeth said, yanking Chelsea's hand.

Chelsea released Elizabeth's hand and teetered on her tiptoes. "No. I want to talk with him. I want to say hi. Come with me," she said.

Elizabeth closed her eyes in resignation and shook her head. "Nope. Because this is a bad idea."

Boyd was quickly disappearing in the throngs of people.

Chelsea started walking backward toward Boyd. "Go get us those doughnuts. I'll catch up with you. I promise."

A minute later, Chelsea stood behind Boyd, her arms folded over her body, her insides jittery. He'd surely be as surprised to see her as she was at seeing him. But how did he feel about her now? He'd tried reaching out to her several times in the weeks and months after the murders, but Chelsea had ignored his calls. She'd been much too raw, much too unstable to talk with him. She'd needed to distance herself from anything to do with that night. It was the whole reason she'd moved to Boston.

Fresh city. Fresh start.

And far enough away from Ethan to feel maybe a little safe.

Over the years she'd wondered how Boyd must have felt, leaving the party before the massacre began. Had he been relieved? Did he have survivor's guilt like she did? Had he been shocked that Ethan could commit murder?

She watched Boyd talk to a man selling dried herbs. He laughed at something the man said, and the sound sent a chill up her spine.

Sweat formed beneath her underarms. Okay, maybe Elizabeth had been right. Maybe this *was* a bad idea.

She started to turn, to head back toward Elizabeth and the two competing stands that sold cider doughnuts. She was in midturn when Boyd spun around and almost walked right into her.

"Oh, sorry," he apologized. He started to move past, but then his ice-blue eyes snapped back to hers and widened. His jaw dropped. "Ch . . . Chelsea?"

He looked like he'd seen a ghost.

"Hi," she said nervously.

"Wow," he said, running his fingers through his thick, dark hair. "Wow. I, uh—" His eyes slid to the scar on her cheek. "Jesus," he muttered and shook his head.

She instinctively raised her hand and touched the scar.

He stared at her, his Adam's apple bobbing. "Sorry, it's just . . ."

Her knees began to weaken, and again she second-guessed her decision.

"Holy shit. I . . . I can't believe it's you. You know, I tried contacting you after, you know, everything."

"I know. I'm sorry."

"Oh, no. I get it. I do." His eyes slipped over her scar again, then quickly circled back to her eyes. "They said on the news that you were hurt really bad. That you almost died. NBC did that special news show on what happened. Did you see it?"

She shifted on her feet. No, she hadn't seen it. And she'd refused to grant the producers an interview. She'd wanted no part of any of it.

His thick brow furrowed. "I'm glad you're okay. I mean, you are. Right?"

Should she tell him that she'd lost many of her memories of that night? That she sometimes felt like she'd lost part of her mind? That she still had awful nightmares and didn't sleep much? Her lips twitched as she attempted to smile. "I have my good days. My bad days. But I'm not complaining. And you?" she asked. "How are you doing?"

For the next few minutes, Boyd gave her a thumbnail sketch of what he'd been doing since that night. He told her he hadn't finished college. That he'd ended up moving back to his hometown of Marblehead. She was familiar with it. It was a nice coastal town about an hour north of Boston. He wound up marrying a girl he'd gone to high school with, but they had separated and were going through a divorce.

"I'm so sorry to hear that."

"Thanks, but it's what's best for both of us. We weren't good together."

"I'm sure it's still been hard. Are you doing okay?" she asked.

"Yeah, sure. I mean, we've been separated almost a year now. The divorce will be final soon."

She nodded. "So, you come to the city often?"

He shook his head. "Never. That's part of what's so wild about this. It's my first trip to Boston in, like, literally, years. I do business development for a chain of car-detailing shops. Fine Brush. Ever hear of it?"

Chelsea shook her head.

"We're not in the city yet. But we will be. I'm here scouting locations for a possible expansion. Oh, that reminds me." He looked down at his watch. "Man, this really sucks. But I have to get going. Gotta meet a Realtor."

She took a step back and tried to conceal her disappointment. "Oh, sure. Okay." Talking to him felt good. She didn't want it to end.

"But we've gotta catch up," he said. "We should grab dinner."

"Yeah," she said and felt a surge of relief.

"Tomorrow night work for you?"

"Yeah. Tomorrow night's great."

Boyd stored her number in his phone and quickly said goodbye, then vanished back into the crowd. As Chelsea went to find Elizabeth, her body was literally vibrating with excitement. She even felt a smile, a real one, spread across her face.

For the first time in a while, Elizabeth had been wrong about something. Saying hello to Boyd hadn't been a bad decision at all. Dinner wouldn't be, either. And even if it was, it was just dinner, so what was the worst that could happen? She'd feel uncomfortable and have to cut it short?

Big deal.

Uncomfortable was her normal. And dinner with Boyd was a risk she was willing to take.

CHAPTER 4

THE NEXT NIGHT a brisk wind sent crisp leaves dancing across the balcony as Chelsea brought her plants inside.

Boyd would be arriving in half an hour. They had dinner reservations for Giulia's at 7:00 p.m. Chelsea's heart fluttered like hummingbird wings as she anticipated his arrival. It wasn't every day that she went to dinner with a friend, especially one as handsome as Boyd. In fact, she couldn't even *remember* the last time. Her social life pretty much consisted of eating microwaveable food in front of the television set with Elizabeth while watching a movie or binge-watching some show.

Back inside her apartment, she brewed some coffee, then went to the bathroom to finish getting ready. Ten minutes later, she heard a knock on the door.

Frowning, she glanced at her watch. If it was Boyd, he was very early. And Elizabeth had a key, so she always let herself in. It was rare that anyone else ever showed up at her door.

She glanced through the peephole and saw Boyd staring back. She took a deep breath and opened the door.

Boyd stood in the doorway, wearing a suede jacket over a button-down flannel shirt and blue jeans. His short, dark hair was gelled in the front, and although his eyes were a little bloodshot, he looked great.

"Hey," he said, out of breath, as though he'd taken the stairs up quickly. He stepped toward her and pulled her into a hug. She tried not to tense beneath his touch, but it had been a long time since anyone had hugged her. Elizabeth wasn't the touchy-feely type, and Chelsea wasn't close enough with anyone else to warrant intimate body contact.

Boyd smelled great. A little earthy and minty, definitely clean. She felt a tiny leap in her chest before pulling away. "Come in," she said, trying to keep her voice even. "You're early."

"I hope it's okay. I thought there'd be more traffic," he said. He walked past her into her small living room.

"Yeah. Of course."

He looked around. "Wow. Great place."

She noticed he was carrying a large black leather bag over one shoulder. "Man purse?"

He turned to her and grinned. "Ha. You're still funny."

I was funny?

She filed away that bit of new information. It was a part of herself that she hadn't remembered. And she liked it.

"I prefer to call it a shoulder bag, thank you," he said with a wide smile. He set the bag down next to the couch. "My car was broken into last week, and now I hate to leave anything important in it." He walked toward the French doors that led to her balcony. "Wow, you have a view, too?"

"Well, it's not the best," she said, standing next to him and peering out at the building next to hers and a sliver of Newbury Street, the Rodeo Drive of Boston. "But at least it's something."

"I think it's great."

"Thanks. Hey, if you don't mind, I need a few more minutes to finish getting ready," she said. "Would you like something to drink? Coffee? Water?"

"I'm good." He turned away from the balcony and settled onto the couch, then grabbed his shoulder bag, unzipped it, and pulled out an iPad.

"Okay. I'll be fast."

She retreated to the bathroom and hurried to put the finishing touches on her makeup. Ten minutes later, she emerged. As she passed through her bedroom, she froze. The bottom drawer of her dresser was ajar. She went to it and checked its contents and noticed that her old college scrapbook, the oldest thing she still had from the first twenty-three years of her life, was missing.

What the . . . ?

Had Boyd been snooping around?

She knew the thought was crazy, but she hadn't been in that drawer for months.

Or had she?

Her memory had been so unreliable since the murders, she couldn't be sure.

She glanced from the drawer to the living room and saw Boyd playing with Harry. She was shocked the cat wasn't hiding. He *always* hid when people came around. Not that anyone but Elizabeth ever did. She watched Boyd dangle a toy in front of the cat and laugh as Harry batted at it.

Boyd noticed her and grinned. "I'm normally not a cat person, but this little guy is hysterical."

She smiled back, then discreetly pushed the drawer shut with her foot.

She'd worry about the scrapbook later.

❀❀❀

The savory scents of roasted garlic and oregano hung in the air at Giulia's.

As soon as they sat down, Boyd ordered a bottle of pinot noir. Chelsea hadn't touched a drop of alcohol since the night of the murders, but her heart was thudding faster than usual, so she decided to let herself have a glass.

The restaurant was small and intimate with deep-red leather chairs and dark-mahogany wood tables. Piano music played softly from hidden speakers. Chelsea looked across the table at Boyd, taking in his blue eyes, strong jaw, and perfectly straight nose and teeth, and realized again how incredibly handsome he was.

"God, there's so much I want to talk about," he said. "I'm not even sure where to start."

She caught his eyes slide across the scar on her cheek again before flickering to the backs of her hands, which were also full of ugly, raised scars. Was he feeling pity for her? She placed her hands in her lap.

She didn't like people to feel sorry for her.

She hated how the media had portrayed her as a victim all those months after the murders. She didn't want others to see her that way. She didn't want to see *herself* that way. She just wanted the nightmare to finally be over, so she could just be Chelsea, whoever the hell that was.

"I'm sorry," he said. "But your scars. I can't get over the fact that he did that to you."

She decided to change the direction of the conversation. "So, how long were you married?" she asked.

"A little over a year. One of the worst years of my life, and that's saying a lot," he said and laughed, but his eyes didn't join in. He grabbed a piece of crusty bread, broke off a piece, then drenched it in olive oil and balsamic vinegar. "The marriage was a big mistake. Of course, I didn't realize it at the time, but it was just a pathetic attempt at having a normal life. Proving I wasn't still a screwup."

A screwup? He didn't appear that way to her at all. "How do you mean?"

Before he could answer, the wine appeared. Chelsea watched as Boyd swirled the wine around a little in the wineglass, smelled it, took a sip, then nodded. The waiter nodded back, filled both glasses one-third of the way, and quietly walked off.

Chelsea sipped her wine while she listened to Boyd explain that he'd had a drug problem in college that got much worse after the murders. He said he'd gone to rehab for it several times over the past four years, and it had caused a big rift between him and his family and most of his friends. Peering into his eyes, which were still a little bloodshot, Chelsea couldn't help but wonder if he'd relapsed again.

"I just finally decided that I needed to get my shit together," he continued. "So I sobered up and asked Lisa to marry me. I was so focused on proving to everyone that I was capable of having a normal life that I didn't even consider that I might not really be ready for marriage."

He glanced down at the table. "It all made perfect sense at the time." His frown deepened. "But, man, I made so many bad decisions. Really bad ones, including agreeing to work for her father. I mean, it should have been obvious that the marriage was doomed from the start."

"Doomed?"

He took a long sip of his wine, then set the glass down. "There was no trust. She knew what I'd gone through with the drugs, so she figured she'd keep a tight leash on me, and I'm not good with leashes. We butted heads and argued. Like, all-the-time argued. And that stressed me out. I ended up relapsing twice, which made things even worse, and we ended up hating each other." His eyes locked on hers. "You know how when you're with someone, how you always look forward to seeing them?"

Chelsea nodded, though she couldn't recall the feeling.

"Well, it was the exact opposite with her."

"Do you still love her?" she asked.

He shook his head. "No. I fell out of love with her a long time ago." He poured them both more wine, and she noticed his hand was trembling a little. "But enough about my marriage."

He set the bottle down and looked up at her, his eyes glinting beneath the soft glow of the candlelight. "I can't even tell you how much that night screwed me up." He shook his head. "I still have trouble believing it sometimes. I mean, Ethan. Who would have thought, right? That he could kill two people in fucking cold blood like that?"

Chelsea wasn't sure how to respond. She looked past Boyd to the piano player and watched as he flipped through his sheet music. The wine was working its way into her bloodstream. She felt warm inside. Looser, more relaxed, even despite the topic of their conversation.

"Jesus. How did I live with someone for two semesters and have no idea he was so messed up?"

She returned her attention to Boyd, remembering again how he'd stared at her the night of the murders, right before he left. She wanted to ask him what he'd been thinking then, but there was no way to ask the question without it sounding weird.

Boyd passed his hand slowly over his mouth, then looked at her. "I have nightmares about that night. Like, all the time."

Me, too. "You do?"

"Yeah."

Knowing he also had nightmares comforted her. Maybe it was because for the first time since everything happened, she realized she wasn't the only one still aching from that night. Obviously, Amy's and Christine's families did. And other people who had loved them. But she didn't let herself think of them too often. Especially Amy's parents, Mr. and Mrs. Harris.

The last time she'd seen them was a week after the murders, at Amy's funeral. A social worker from the psychiatric hospital had brought her, but Chelsea had ended up leaving just fifteen minutes after arriving.

As soon as she walked into the church, Mrs. Harris had recognized her. She'd left her position by Amy's closed casket and rushed past everyone to get to her. She'd grasped her bandaged wrists tightly, too tightly, and yanked her down so they were sitting next to each other on the last row of wooden benches, then sobbed on her shoulder. It was as though the woman thought that being close to her would somehow bring her closer to her dead daughter.

People had watched and whispered as Chelsea sat trapped by Mrs. Harris. Then finally Mr. Harris had sat down and whispered into Mrs. Harris's ear. When the woman didn't let her go, he tried to coax her to release Chelsea's hand. But she wouldn't. He had to physically pry her hand open so Chelsea could escape.

After that horrible experience, Chelsea had decided not to go to Christine's funeral, which was scheduled for the next afternoon. Since that day, Chelsea had tried not to think about their families at all. It was too painful.

"Jesus, would you listen to me?" Boyd said. "I'm sitting here talking about myself when *you* were the one in the freaking middle of it. You almost died. God, I'm sorry. I can be such an asshole."

"No. It's okay. You know, I know it sounds awful, but it's good to know I'm not the only one still screwed up from that night."

Boyd stared at her. "That's exactly how I feel."

They lapsed into silence for a moment; then Boyd's mouth suddenly spread into a smile. She noticed that it warmed her insides even more than the wine. "So, how have you been?" he asked. "Like, truthfully."

She glanced past him, her eyes taking in the piano player again, unsure how much she wanted to tell him. On the one hand, she had the desire to unload. To just purge and lay everything on the table, see what he thought about it all: the amnesia, imagining she saw Ethan around every corner, the terrible nightmares, her constant thoughts of suicide, and the occasional blackouts. But on the other hand, she didn't want to scare him away or, maybe even worse, make him feel pity for her.

"I still struggle, but things are mostly good."

"Do you keep in touch with anyone from college?" he asked.

She shrugged. "A couple of girls who I used to study with visited me in the hospital. But that was the last I saw or heard from them."

"No one else?"

She shook her head.

"How well did you know them? Amy and Christine?"

Chelsea suddenly got a flash of their faces. Amy's pale, freckled skin and straight auburn hair, her mouth always spread into a smile. Christine's alabaster skin, silky blonde hair, and ridiculously long, dark lashes. They'd both been attractive, intelligent, and kind, and probably would have had long, happy lives. She still had no clue why Ethan would want to kill them. Any of them.

"I just met them that semester after answering an ad for a room, so not that well. Did you know them?"

He shook his head. "No. That night was the first time I met them."

He reached out and touched her hand, surprising her and making her breath catch. He glided his index finger slowly along the many raised scars on the back of her hand, and every nerve ending in her body tingled. "I still can't believe you went through all of that," he said. "Only a monster could do that to you. To anyone."

Tears welled up in her eyes. She wasn't exactly sure why. Maybe it was from his understanding, the kindness of his touch. Or maybe the acceptance she felt from him despite all her hideous scars. She looked down at the table and struggled to hold the tears back.

"You okay?" he asked.

"Yeah."

"You sure?"

She looked up at him and nodded. "Yeah, I'm good."

He squeezed her hand, released it, and sat back in his chair. "They said you blocked out what happened that night. Is that true?"

She sniffed. "They?"

"The media."

"Oh. Yeah. They diagnosed me with something called psychogenic amnesia. People sometimes get it after experiencing trauma. It's a way for the mind to protect itself, I guess."

"So, what kind of things can't you remember?"

"Most of that night, but even stuff before it. Like, most of my childhood. It's so strange. The only thing I remember somewhat clearly is that semester of college, up to that night . . . and that's still not perfect. If I try hard to remember anything else, I always end up with a migraine. But thankfully it doesn't affect new memories."

At least, I don't think it does.

It surprised her to hear herself telling him all this. She certainly hadn't planned to. Maybe she'd needed to talk about it to someone other than Elizabeth. She didn't like talking with Elizabeth about that night, about its lingering effects on her. Not that Elizabeth wouldn't listen. She would. And she did. But Elizabeth was so strong, Chelsea always felt a little ashamed to talk too much about her problems.

There was awe in his eyes. "Wow. That's crazy. Do you think you'll ever get it all back?"

"I don't know." She looked down at her wine. "It's part of the reason why I don't usually drink. Since everything happened, I have this almost-obsessive need to always be in control."

He glanced at her wineglass. "Oh, shit. I'm sorry. I didn't even think to ask."

She was relieved he was more concerned about the wine than what she'd told him. Relieved that he wasn't treating her like a freak for having issues, which, in that moment, made her see herself as a little less freakish.

She now understood why she'd had such a powerful urge to approach him at the farmers' market. She'd wanted a friend who she could talk with about that night. One who could truly understand the horror of what had happened.

"No, it's okay. I feel good right now. Maybe I should do this more often. Let go a bit."

"Yeah, maybe." He smiled.

She could tell he understood. Of course he did, because he was in pain, too. Boyd was another damaged soul from that terrible night. A kindred spirit. It was refreshing to be around someone else who was damaged and wasn't afraid to admit to it.

She looked up and saw that Boyd was staring at her. But this time he wasn't studying her scars. He was looking at *her*. "I'm so glad we ran into each other," he said.

"I'm glad we did, too."

Later, after they had said their goodbyes and she was getting ready for bed, Chelsea realized she was smiling again. She hadn't smiled this much in . . . honestly, she had no idea. She just knew that she felt lighter, as if she had shrugged off one of the oppressive blankets that had been weighing her down for the last several years.

She went to her dresser to grab a nightgown, and for the first time since they'd left the apartment for dinner, she remembered the scrapbook.

The smile melted from her lips.

Don't do this.

You're being paranoid.

What would he want with an old scrapbook?

She considered searching for the scrapbook or calling Elizabeth to ask if she'd seen it. But it was late, so she tried to push it to the back of her mind for now.

After brushing her teeth and washing her face, she climbed into bed, switched off her bedside lamp, and closed her eyes. She replayed dinner. Boyd had made her feel normal, even if she wasn't. Not since the murders. Normal people didn't have memories that had been erased. They didn't have blackouts. They had family and friends who cared about them, who showed up at the hospital when they were in critical condition after being found carved up and left for dead.

Chelsea didn't have any of those things. But Boyd didn't seem to care. At least, he didn't tonight.

She sank deep beneath her heavy covers, thinking about Boyd, and felt an excited fluttering in her belly. It had felt great connecting with him, not feeling afraid, and letting her guard down for once.

CHAPTER 5

CHELSEA OPENED HER eyes the next morning and instantly knew something was different. Then she recognized what it was.

Sunlight was streaming through her window.

The sun was never out when she woke up. She looked at her bedside clock: 7:47 a.m. She'd slept four hours longer than usual. She hadn't slept this long for months. She also realized she hadn't had the nightmare. It was the first time in more than a year.

Outside, the chilly autumn-morning air was invigorating. She took a deep breath as she started on her route. For the first mile, she cleared her mind, concentrating on her pace as she ran, listening to her footsteps pound the cold concrete sidewalk. On her second mile, she let her mind drift back to last night.

Dinner with Boyd had been positive.

Therapeutic.

Was that why she hadn't had the nightmare?

It had felt so good to talk to him. And not just about the murders. She had enjoyed his company. His easy laugh. She remembered the tingling sensation she'd felt when he'd run his fingertip across the scars on the back of her hand. She was hopeful that there would be more dinners. More chances to connect with him. Maybe she should start making more friends. Maybe she was ready for that now.

After the murders, she'd needed her life quiet, stable, and predictable to be able to heal. So, for years, she did little besides run, work, and stay home. Elizabeth joined her on the nights she was free, but that was usually only a few nights a week. The rest of the time she spent by herself with Harry. But dinner with Boyd had shown her that maybe now she was ready for something more. Maybe she was ready to make her world a little bigger.

As she crossed the street, she suddenly felt the sensation of someone watching her. The hairs on her arms sprang up, her mind flashing to an image of Ethan. She whirled around so fast, her ponytail whipped her across her face and made her eyes water. But no one was behind her. Just a passing city bus and a woman walking her small dog.

She'd just imagined it.

Like she always did.

As she neared her apartment, she took a small detour to the park a few blocks from her building and sprinted through the empty playground, the wood chips crunching beneath her feet. She jogged up a sharp incline. By the time she reached the top of the grassy hill, her thighs were on fire. She lay on the ground, trying to catch her breath. She pushed her hands out to her sides and raked her fingers through the cold, soft blades of grass, letting them tickle the skin between her fingers.

Had she done this when she was a child? A teenager? She sometimes wished she could remember more about those years.

After a long moment, she sat up and gazed out at the languid, peaceful Charles River in the distance. Then she looked up at the sky, letting the sun warm her face.

This was going to be a good day.

❖❖❖

BACK AT HER apartment, she brewed a pot of coffee, then went to the bathroom and peeled off her clothes. She let the hot spray of the shower thunder down on her body, pelt every inch of her skin. She turned to let it hit her face and felt the blood immediately rush to her forehead, her cheeks, her chin.

She had to go to the office this morning. She worked as a medical transcriptionist—a job that afforded her the ability to work primarily from home and also enjoy a comfortable living. Her agency, which serviced clients like doctors and independent scientists, would send her reports in audio files, and Chelsea would convert them into text formats. The job kept her busy, which, for her, was crucial.

Most days she could receive the files that needed transcribing electronically. But today's audio files needed to be picked up in person because a client was experiencing technical issues. She'd agreed to stop by the office to get them. She hated going to the office. She much preferred staying at home and working in her pajamas or yoga pants, but it was part of the job, and she needed to eat. Besides, she was rarely required to venture out of her apartment for work more than once a month, so she could hardly complain.

As she toweled off from her shower, she studied her naked body in the full-length mirror. Scars from the stab wounds marred her olive skin, making her look and feel more like a science experiment than a woman. She ran her fingers over the many physical reminders of that night.

Even though Elizabeth had thought it was too soon, Chelsea had decided a year after the murders to order her file from the Department of Children and Families, hoping she could piece her past together. She'd learned she'd lived with eight different foster families before the age of eighteen. She'd tried to contact a caseworker she'd had for six of those years, to see what she could tell her, but the woman had already retired. Chelsea had gone so far as to visit one of the foster families with whom she'd lived, but it had been a negative experience. It was at that point she decided she would just start anew. With a blank slate. At least, for now.

Golden light from the morning sun flooded in through the French doors that led to her balcony as she poured a second cup of coffee into her favorite ceramic mug. She slipped on her fleece jacket, grabbed her keys, and soldiered out the door. While she walked through the hallway that led to the stairwell, her phone buzzed. It was a text from Boyd.

Still thinking about our dinner last night. We need to do it again soon.

Her stomach did a little flip. She smiled as she thumbed a reply.

I'd like that.

Little thought bubbles instantly appeared on her screen, letting her know he was typing another message. She waited in anticipation.

How about this weekend?

She grinned and quickly agreed.

Pushing open the door at the bottom of the stairwell, she felt a little giddy. Now outside, she curled her fingers around her pepper spray and made her way toward her silver Toyota Tercel, which was parked on the street a block away. As she neared her car, she thought she could see a slip of paper under her wiper blade.

Great. Another ticket.

She hadn't thought she'd left her car in a no-parking zone, but honestly, the city seemed to change the zoning daily. Who could keep up?

As she got closer, she saw it wasn't a ticket at all. It was a note. She grabbed it, and as her eyes slipped over the message, an icicle of panic sliced through her heart. Her mug slipped from her fingers and shattered on the asphalt.

❖ ❖ ❖

Fifteen minutes later, Chelsea's heart was still stuttering inside her chest.

Elizabeth sat across from her, staring at the note.

"It's probably just a prank. Someone found out where you live. Some asshole with too much time on his hands."

Chelsea wrung her moist hands. The message had been written with a red marker.

YOU MADE ME

It was the same message that had been scrawled on the bathroom mirror the night of the murders.

Chelsea shook her head. "No one knows about that message. The police never released it to the public."

Elizabeth shrugged. "It's been almost five years. Maybe someone leaked it at some point. Things like that happen all the time."

Chelsea wasn't convinced. It had to have been Ethan. He was back, and chances were he truly had been around her at least one, if not several, of the times when she'd thought she'd seen him. But then another possibility popped into her head, and she felt a sick sensation in the pit of her gut.

Boyd. Could he have . . . ?

After all, the timing was too . . .

But no. It couldn't have been him. He would've had to have known about the message left the night of the murders, and the only way he could possibly know that was if Elizabeth had been right and the information had been leaked.

That, or if he'd talked to Ethan since that night.

She circled back to how raw and genuine Boyd had seemed during dinner. How honest, kind.

No, he wouldn't have done that.

It was Ethan.

It's always been Ethan.

Elizabeth arched an eyebrow. "Do you think that your friend Boyd could have left it? After all—"

Chelsea shook her head, not ready to admit that the thought had crossed her mind, too. Elizabeth said something else, but Chelsea had stopped listening. White noise flooded her mind as she drifted back to that night. To everyone drinking and having fun. To her feeling queasy, Ethan trying to feel her up, Christine and Amy dancing in the middle of the living room, the little mouse scurrying across the kitchen floor. The scents of whiskey, pizza, cigarette smoke. To everything fading to black, and then waking up in the bathtub freezing and in gut-wrenching pain.

"Chels, you're white as a ghost." Elizabeth pressed the back of her hand to Chelsea's forehead. "You should lie down."

Elizabeth pulled her to her feet and led her toward her bedroom.

"I should call the police."

"Yes, but take a few minutes to calm down first. You don't want to have one of your blackouts."

Elizabeth was right. She hadn't suffered a blackout in almost a year, and stress always brought them on. And once she began blacking out, she tended to spiral quickly in the wrong direction. She couldn't let that happen.

"The office. They're expecting me. I can't not go—"

"Okay. Here's what we're going to do," Elizabeth said. "You're going to lie down, and I'll go pick the stuff up for you. Give me the address, and stop worrying about it. Just focus on relaxing for a few minutes."

Elizabeth helped her into bed and sat beside her, pulling a pill bottle from her nightstand drawer. She shook two Valium out and handed her a glass of water. "Take these, and try to relax. I'll be back in less than an hour."

This was exactly what she needed. Elizabeth in full take-charge mode. Both as a nurse and as a friend. As much as Chelsea didn't want to continue to rely on her, it felt good that she could, at least for now.

Her blood still electric, she swallowed the pills. Then she lay on her side and replayed finding the note and seeing the guy sitting in his car just a few mornings earlier and thinking it had been Ethan. She'd been right, after all.

But then Boyd's face flashed into her mind, and she winced. As unlikely as it was that he had left the note, she couldn't totally discount the possibility.

She wouldn't think about that now. Elizabeth was right. She needed to try to calm down. She pushed her thoughts to the back of her mind and closed her eyes.

CHAPTER 6

ROBERT LANG'S STOMACH growled as the scents of beef and garlic wafted through the living room's air vents and into his nostrils. He was playing with his three-year-old grandson, Nicky, while his daughter, Victoria, cooked dinner in the next room.

Waiting for dinner to be ready, he batted a red balloon high into the air. Nicky squealed, then took off running after it. When his phone rang, Lang looked at the incoming number.

Boston area code.

He frowned, wondering who it could be. Nicky handed the balloon to him. He batted it in the air again and watched Nicky chase it again with delight, then accepted the call.

"Lang here."

A beat of silence, then: "*Detective* Lang?"

No one had called him that in a while. "Retired."

Lang had retired at thirty-eight as a result of a car accident. Luckily he'd been on duty at the time, which qualified him to collect a good pension. It was generous enough to ensure he wouldn't have to work again, if he didn't want to. But he did. Last week he'd signed on to work part-time, reviewing some of the Springfield PD's cold-case files.

Going back to work wasn't about the money. His needs were few. He just needed to stay busy and get back to doing the job he loved.

Detective work was in his blood. He'd become antsy sitting around at his daughter's house, watching Nicky and shuttling back and forth to various rehab appointments. There were only so many jigsaw puzzles he could assemble at home. He needed to be out in the field. He needed to be challenged, get his sense of purpose back—and the only job that had ever awarded him a sense of satisfaction was being a detective.

"How can I help you?" he asked, taking the balloon from Nicky. He pressed his index finger to his lips to let the little boy know he should be quiet before tossing it high in the air again.

"Lang, this is Detective Roy Garcia, Boston PD. Your station gave me your number."

He watched Nicky barrel down the hallway and vanish into his bedroom. A second later the bedroom door slammed. "What can I do for you, Detective?"

"You headed up the Springfield Coed Killings five years ago, right?"

"That's correct. At least, initially."

"You remember Chelsea Dutton, the survivor?"

Of course he remembered Chelsea. She'd been gravely injured when he and a young officer had discovered her in the apartment's hallway bathroom. And she had haunted his dreams ever since.

Something about the young woman had touched him. It wasn't only sympathy for the young survivor of such a grisly crime, but something more personal. Maybe it was because Chelsea Dutton had reminded him of his daughter. They had the same dark hair and olive skin, and they were very close in age. But while Victoria had made the somewhat common mistake of getting involved with a man who didn't love her and getting pregnant at a young age, Chelsea Dutton had made the mistake of inviting the wrong guy into her apartment, who'd ended up killing her roommates and leaving her at death's door. Or maybe it was the fact that Chelsea had had very few visitors at the hospital as she'd fought for her life in the intensive-care unit. Only two friends, fellow students of hers from Springfield, had visited her. Girls who had been in her study group.

He remembered the first time he'd walked into Chelsea's room in the intensive-care unit and had seen how bare it was. No get-well balloons. No stuffed animals. So he'd gone down to the gift shop and bought her some. The second day into the investigation, he'd sat at her bedside for about thirty minutes, hoping that someone would show. But no one had. She'd been pale and frightened and struggling to make sense of everything that had happened to her and her friends. Confused, she kept asking him, "Why would he do this?" and "Why did he kill them and not me?"

The third day into the investigation, Chelsea had crawled out of her hospital bed, found a pair of surgical scissors, and opened her wrists.

Once she had been stabilized physically, she had been transferred to a local psychiatric hospital and put on a three-month hold. He had been en route to the hospital when he'd heard. But not five minutes after receiving the call, an SUV had hit him head-on. He'd sustained a lumbar spinal fracture and a fractured patella and spent the next four years in and out of surgeries and rehab and on various drugs for pain management.

It had always disturbed him that the case had gotten away from him and gone cold. That the two dead girls, Dutton, and the families involved had never received justice. That the department had failed them. Not that it was so unusual.

Lang's gut told him that Detective Duplechaine, who had taken over the investigation after his accident, hadn't exhausted all the leads. Not that Duplechaine wasn't a competent detective. But detectives, like everyone else, were human and often made mistakes, especially when their units were short-staffed, as theirs was at the time.

"Dutton found a note on her vehicle this morning," Garcia was saying on the other end of the line. He went on to tell Lang the circumstances. When Lang heard what the note had said, he understood why Garcia was calling him.

The message on the bathroom mirror the night of the murders had been classified. Other than law enforcement at the scene and the crime-scene investigators, no one had known there'd ever been a message, let alone what it had said. No one, of course, but the person who'd left it.

The bedroom door flew open, and Nicky shot out into the hallway, then back into the living room. He climbed up on the couch and leaped to the recliner.

"Our understanding here is that the key suspect in the Springfield Coed Killings was a man named Ethan Klebold," Detective Garcia continued. "But he was never taken into custody, and the case ended up cold."

"That's affirmative."

Garcia filled him in on the incident that happened in Boston earlier that day and asked a few more questions. When they hung up, Lang called his supervisor at Springfield PD and told him what had happened.

Then he carried Nicky into the kitchen, where Victoria was preparing Lang's favorite dinner: meatloaf, asparagus roasted in garlic butter, and a Caesar salad.

He switched off Victoria's country music and situated twenty-five-pound Nicky into his high chair. As he set the boy down, a bolt of pain lit up his back. Even after all the surgeries and physical therapy, his back and knee were still in bad shape. If it were up to him, he would discontinue therapy. It seemed pointless. But Victoria insisted on it. Victoria insisted on a lot of things. And as infuriating as that was, it didn't make him love her any less.

Victoria turned, licking a wooden spoon. "Who was on the phone?"

"Boston PD," Lang said. He grabbed Nicky's favorite Elmo bib and fastened it around his neck.

Victoria's brows met in the middle. "Oh?"

"Something's come up. I'll probably be in Boston for a little while."

Concern creased her face. "What? Why?"

Lang pulled out silverware and began setting the table. "There's been a new development in an old case."

"Is everything okay?"

Chelsea Dutton's face flashed into his mind. The mere thought of her being in danger again seemed so wrong, almost obscene. "I hope so."

CHAPTER 7

CHELSEA SAT BUNDLED up on her balcony and watched as a storm slowly rolled into the city.

Breathing in the scent of ozone and roasting meat from an apartment nearby, she replayed everything that had happened the day before. A Detective Garcia and an officer whose name she couldn't remember had shown up and taken her statement and the note, then said they'd get back to her in a day or two. She'd tried to get some work done a few times since waking that morning, but she couldn't get Ethan off her mind. Now she was almost certain he was out there somewhere, watching her. Her veins went icy just thinking about it.

When the wind on the balcony became too strong, she retreated inside her apartment and made a mug of hot cocoa, then sat on her couch and listened to the howling wind shake the windowpanes.

Her phone buzzed.

It was a text from Boyd.

Would you like company Friday?

Seeing his name, she felt her heart lift a little. But then she thought about the note again. She reminded herself that it was extremely unlikely that he even knew about the message left on the mirror that night. And if he didn't know about the message, he couldn't have possibly left the note.

You're just being paranoid.

Stop.

The timing is simply a coincidence.

She sank down deep into the couch and thumbed:

Found a creepy note on my car yesterday.

She pressed "Send."

Five seconds later, thought bubbles popped up, and she replied.

Creepy? What did it say?

You made me.

U made me what?

I don't know.

That's strange. Who do u think left it?

I'm not sure. Ethan maybe?

What? R u serious? Why would u think it would be him?

Should she tell him that it had been the same message left the night of the murders? She knew the information had been confidential five years ago, but was it now? She decided to ask Lang before saying anything.

I called the cops. They're checking into it.

OK, good. Are you OK?

I'm fine.

As she waited for his reply again, she suddenly felt the sensation of someone watching her. Dread curling in her chest, she jumped up and peered through the French doors to see if there was anyone on the street below.

A streak of lightning sliced across the sky as she scanned Dartmouth Street and the little bit of Newbury Street she could see.

There was nobody there.

She watched for several minutes, until the rain began coming down in sheets. Then she double-checked the lock on the French doors.

She was about to pull her curtains closed when there was a knock on the door.

❋ ❋ ❋

Lang knocked on the door of Chelsea Dutton's apartment, glad to see that she was living in a nice building in a safe neighborhood.

He heard footsteps approach from inside, then silence.

A soft voice asked: "Detective Lang?"

"Yes, ma'am."

He heard a door chain disengage, then a lock turn. Then another. When Chelsea Dutton finally opened the door, he was immediately transported back to the scene of the slayings. To the image of her cowering in the bathtub like a wounded animal, looking like death itself. Then to the confused, sorrowful girl that lay in the hospital bed afterward, asking so many questions that he still couldn't answer.

She looked different now. Not only was it obvious she'd grown older; her whole countenance was different. She looked confident, not meek. Her pallid color had been replaced with a warmer tone, her cheeks had a healthy flush, and the dark circles beneath her eyes had all but disappeared. The only visible sign of that night was a nasty scar on her cheek that extended from the side of her nose to her left ear.

"Oh, my God," she said. "I can't believe it's really you."

He'd hoped his visit wouldn't be upsetting. "I hope it's okay. I was going to call—"

"No. It's totally fine. Is this about the note? Did Detective Garcia call you?"

"Yes, ma'am. To both."

She moved aside to let him in. "Come in. Please." A smile spread across her face, revealing perfect teeth.

He realized this was the first time he'd seen her smile.

She took his umbrella, then moved aside so he could enter. He walked in and made mental notes as he surveyed her small third-floor apartment. The place was both feminine and cozy, and the savory scent of bacon grease hung in the air, making his stomach growl. The coffee he had picked up at a gas station on his way to see her had been anything but satisfying.

Her furnishings were sparse but comfortable. An overstuffed white couch sat against the far wall of the living room. A collection of yellow throw pillows and colorful knickknacks brightened the room even more. French doors afforded a nice view.

"Can I get you something to drink?" she asked. "I have hot cocoa."

He shook his head. "No, thank you."

"Okay, well, then please have a seat." She motioned to the couch. "I'll just be a second."

He watched her disappear into the kitchen and took the extra time to look around a little more. The place was very clean, tidy and bright. There was a desk in the corner of the living room. A cat walked out from beneath it, stared at him, and meowed.

"Hi, kitty," he said. He thought about bending to pet it but figured it would be a bad idea.

On top of the desk was a laptop, a few files, and a potted rosemary plant. Several sketches had been taped up on the wall above it. He moved closer to see them. "You draw these?" he called.

She reappeared holding a mug of steaming cocoa. He noticed pink slash marks on the backs of her hands and the little bit of her forearms that were exposed below the sleeves of her blue sweatshirt.

She glanced up at the sketches. "Yeah. They're just doodles. Drawing helps me relax."

"You're talented."

She looked pleased.

"Really? You think so?"

"I do. They look like they're all of the same place."

"Yeah."

"Somewhere you know?"

"I'm not sure. It's probably just an image stuck in my head from a magazine," she said. "But my memory is still a mess, so . . ." She shrugged. "Yeah. Who knows?"

Her posture straight, she walked to the other side of the living room. He watched her fold her slender body onto the couch.

"Crazy weather out there, isn't it?" she said, pointing her chin toward the balcony.

"It sure is," he said, lowering himself onto her recliner. His back throbbed something fierce, and he tried not to groan out loud. The drive to Boston had been grueling on his back and knee.

"We've been getting a lot of it lately. More than we usually do this time of year," she said. The cat jumped up on the couch and took a seat in her lap. It eyeballed him. "God, I'm so surprised to see you. It must mean Detective Garcia is taking the note seriously."

"Yes, ma'am, he is. We both are."

"I'm so glad," she said, her eyes shining. She was tearing up.

"So, how are you these days?"

She smiled again. "Better than I was last time I saw you."

He realized she looked even more like Victoria when she smiled. "I'm happy to see you looking so good."

"Thank you."

"So, how bad is it these days? The amnesia?" he asked.

Chelsea's mouth turned down a little at the corners. "My memory isn't much different from before. I remember bits and pieces of stuff here and there. But not much."

"That must be frustrating."

"Yeah. It's really confusing."

"What kinds of things have you been able to remember?"

She shrugged. "A lot of stuff from my past. Like people's faces mostly. Places that I think I might have lived. Nothing that makes a lot of sense, though, really."

"Are you in touch with any of your foster families? Friends from before the killings?"

"No, not really. I did visit this one family a few years ago. The Duvalls. I lived with them for about six months, right before my semester at Springfield. But I mostly know that because I have a copy of my DCF file."

"Oh, good. I'm glad you were able to reconnect."

She shrugged. "Well, it didn't go so great."

"Why's that?"

She explained that after she'd reached out to them, they'd invited her to dinner at their house in Longmeadow, just south of Springfield, but it had been awkward. "They were nice, but they seemed very distracted while I was there. They had their hands full with two young foster kids who kept interrupting, like kids do, I guess. But even if they hadn't, it wasn't like we had much to talk about."

A jagged streak of lightning sliced through the dark sky outside; then thunder boomed, rattling the windowpanes. He watched Chelsea flinch. The cat stood up and stretched, then jumped down from her lap and sniffed Lang's legs.

Chelsea repositioned herself, tucked her feet beneath her body. "I know from my file that I wasn't the best-behaved kid when I lived with them, so maybe it was that. Or maybe they were weirded out by my scars. Or the murders." She shrugged. "Maybe they were afraid my bad luck would rub off on them? Yeah . . . who knows? But they seemed relieved when I said I had to go. So I didn't call them again. And I didn't hear from them, either."

"I'm sorry to hear that."

"Yeah, well. It is what it is, I suppose."

"Have you been in touch with any of the other families who fostered you?"

"No. After that night, I decided to put all that on hold. At least, for now."

He nodded his understanding. He knew from her DCF file that she'd had a terrible childhood. It was probably not a bad thing that she couldn't remember all of it. He'd hoped, though, that she had reconnected with a few people. That she had a support system and was no longer so alone.

The cat jumped into Lang's lap and meowed. "And the night of the attacks? Any new memories at all?" he asked, scratching the cat behind the ears.

She shook her head. "Nothing. I'm sorry. I've tried."

Thunder rumbled again, but this time she didn't flinch. "Did you see the note?" she asked.

"Yeah. I stopped to see Garcia before I came here."

"What do you think? It's Ethan, right?"

"It's very possible, but I'm afraid it's too early to say for sure. Boston PD sent the note off to match the handwriting and check fingerprints."

"And?"

"Nothing's come back yet. It'll probably take a couple of days."

"But I thought no one else knew about the message left in the bathroom. Wasn't it confidential?"

"You're right. But unfortunately, information like that has a way of leaking, especially over time, so we want to rule out other possibilities."

"So I shouldn't tell anyone?"

"I'd strongly advise you not to."

"Okay." She frowned, as though confused. "So, did you drive up here just to see the note?"

"I wanted to see the note, yes. But I'm also reinvestigating your roommates' deaths."

Chelsea's eyes brightened. "Really? You're reopening the case?"

"Well, it was never closed. It just went cold. But yes, I'm here to go through everything again with fresh eyes. Starting at ground zero."

Tears glistened in her eyes, and she wiped at her nose. "I'm . . . so happy to hear that. I really need you to find him."

"Well, I'm going to do everything in my power to try. I'm going back to square one. And that includes reinterviewing everyone, so I'd love to get another statement from you telling me everything you remember. Think you could go over that night for me again?"

"Absolutely."

For the next few minutes, Chelsea recounted everything she remembered as the cat dozed on Lang's lap. He wrote furiously as she told him about the party and the people who had been there. Unfortunately, as she had warned him, these details seemed to amount to no more than she'd been able to give them years ago.

When she was finished, he asked, "Did Detective Duplechaine tell you that Ethan's DNA was found on Christine's body?"

Chelsea's eyes narrowed. "What do you mean?"

"His semen was found. Apparently the two had intercourse that night."

Her brows knitted together. "Oh, wow. That's . . ." She trailed off as though she was processing the information, then shook her head. "No, he didn't say anything about that . . . but I guess I'm not that surprised. He was like that. A pretty big player."

"Do you know if they had any history together? Him and Christine?"

"No. I don't think so. As far as I know, I introduced them that night."

He took down the notes.

"So, how's the rest of your health?" he asked.

"My body still aches sometimes, and I have some nerve damage in my left arm, my hand," she said, stretching out her hand, opening and closing it. "Nothing crazy, though. Thankfully, I'm right-handed, and my liver healed just fine. I could definitely be worse."

A memory of Christine Douglas's and Amy Harris's bodies flashed into his mind.

Yes, she could, he thought.

Much worse.

"Has Ethan ever reached out to you? Since that night?"

Chelsea stopped drinking her cocoa, midsip. "Except the note? No."

Lang asked a few more questions, then stood and handed Chelsea his card. "Like I said, I'm going to be here in Boston for a little while, looking into things. Until we know more, just be vigilant. Keep your doors locked, and don't go anywhere alone after dark until we get to the bottom of this, okay?"

"Okay."

"And if you get nervous being here alone, maybe you can stay with a friend. Or have someone stay here with you."

"I'll do that."

"And if you need anything, anything at all, don't hesitate to call me."

"Okay." She seemed like she wanted to say something but was hesitating.

"Was there something else?"

"Yeah. Do you remember Boyd Lawson? Ethan's roommate?"

"Of course."

"I ran into him a few days ago. It was the first time I've seen him since that night."

CHAPTER 8

CHELSEA LAY ON the couch and thought about Detective Lang's visit the other night. Although she would have thought seeing him again would have been upsetting, it had been surprisingly cathartic. Maybe it was because Lang held a sense of familiarity for her—something she hadn't known she'd been longing for. It was the same thing that had made her approach Boyd.

Plus, she trusted Lang, which was saying a lot for her. Maybe it was the way he listened. Like, *really* listened, without discounting anything. His sharp, watchful eyes steady and unwavering, as though he was interested in everything she said. But, of course, he was. He had a case to investigate.

When she'd first opened the door for him, she'd been surprised by how intense her reaction to him had been. It had been difficult not to reach out and hug him. The more she thought about it, the more her reaction made sense. He had saved her life. If he and the other police officer hadn't arrived when they had, she would have bled out and died.

Rolling off the couch, she went to the bathroom to take a shower. Boyd was coming over tonight. When she'd texted him about the note, he'd seemed concerned, but all he knew was that someone left a strange note. He didn't understand the full gravity of it all. That it was connected to the attack.

She ran the shower and undressed. As she washed, she pushed all thoughts of the note to the back of her mind and let herself wonder how the night would play out. If she'd continue to enjoy Boyd's company as much as before. If he'd continue to enjoy hers.

After her shower, she wiped steam from the bathroom mirror and studied her face. The scar on her cheek looked as intense as always, but there was a brightness in her eyes she couldn't remember seeing for a long time. Maybe ever.

Two hours later, Boyd arrived with Chinese takeout. When he showed up at the door, he looked concerned. "You doing okay?" he asked, setting down the bags. He folded her into a hug.

"Yeah, I'm fine," she said, her stomach doing a flip-flop. She inhaled his scent. Tonight he smelled soapy, minty.

He pulled away to look at her. "You sure?"

She nodded. "I'm good."

"Still creeped out?" he asked, raising his eyebrows.

"Yeah. A little bit."

"And you're being careful?"

She was touched that he was concerned. "Yep."

"Good." He smiled. He turned and grabbed two bottles of wine from one of the bags and held them up. "I wasn't sure if these would be okay. If not, I can always take them back to my car."

"No. It's great," she said, showing him in. "You've successfully corrupted me."

He laughed as he sauntered to the kitchen. "Well, far be it from me to ignore a chance to corrupt a beautiful woman."

Heat rushed to her cheeks. The guy seemed to be the complete package: attractive, intelligent, charming, funny, successful. How could she have not noticed him as much in college? She bet his soon-to-be-ex wife really missed him. How could she not?

They unpacked the food together, and he uncorked a bottle of wine.

"So, where's the note?" he asked, filling their wineglasses.

"I don't have it. The police took it."

"Oh, right," he said, handing her a glass of wine.

He went to the living room and set down his plate. "You made me," he said, repeating the message that had been written on the note. "What the hell does that even mean? You made me *what?*"

She shrugged. "I wish I knew." Being in the same room with Boyd again, watching him try to decode the note, the little suspicion she'd had of him dissolved. It was clear that he was genuinely confused. Either that, or he was one hell of a liar.

Again, she wanted to tell him that the same message had been written on the mirror the night of the murders, but she couldn't.

"You made me," he muttered again, staring at the coffee table, still mulling it over.

She realized that she wanted to talk about anything but that message. Or that night. "Hey, do you mind if we talk about something else for a little while?"

He looked up at her. "Yeah, yeah. Of course. I'm sorry," he said and stabbed a broccoli floret with his fork.

"You don't have to apologize. It's just . . . sometimes it gets to be too much, and I need to think about other things. *Normal* things. Not about murder, nightmares, creepy notes."

"I get it. I should have been more sensitive."

"You are very sensitive. Seriously, I can't tell you how good it's been to be able to talk about all of this stuff with someone who really gets it."

He spooned lo mein noodles on their plates. "You know what you need right now? A good distraction. And, fortunately for you, I am very good at providing that very thing."

She felt herself relax a little. "Yeah? Corruption. Distraction. Those are some admirable traits."

"Yep, I'm pretty much an all-around asshole."

She doubted that. She looked into his kind eyes, and her heart fluttered.

"Thank you," she said.

"For what? Being an asshole?"

"No. For understanding. And for being here."

"Trust me," he said. "There's nowhere else in the world I'd rather be."

❀ ❀ ❀

They enjoyed dinner and the first bottle of wine, then uncorked the second and listened to music. They didn't talk as much as they had over dinner, but there was something very comfortable about their silence. Chelsea found herself feeling more at ease with him than she could ever remember having felt with anyone, even her best friend.

That was not to say she didn't enjoy her time with Elizabeth. Elizabeth was amazing, but she was so together *despite* the difficulties she'd had in her own life, which sometimes made Chelsea feel a little intimidated. With Boyd, she felt like she was on a more even playing field. Also, when she was with him, she felt oddly free of the black cloud that had hovered over her since the attacks, painting the world darker than it probably should be.

After a little while, Boyd reached for her hand and brought it to his mouth. He softly, slowly kissed her scars, making every nerve ending in her body tingle.

"You don't think they're ugly?"

"What? Your scars?"

She nodded.

"God. Of course not."

She studied him.

"I'm serious," he said. "I always thought you were beautiful. One of the most beautiful women I'd ever seen. But you know what?"

"What?"

"You're even more beautiful now."

She cocked her head. "How's that?"

"You really don't get it, do you?"

No, she didn't.

"Chelsea, you survived something awful. Something that would have killed most people. If not physically, then mentally. And you not only survived; you're doing incredible. You have a good job, a great apartment. You have a fantastic head on your shoulders, despite everything that's happened. You're kind, not cynical. It's all a testament to how strong you are. How could anyone not admire you and think you're absolutely incredible?"

She studied his eyes, again searching for a red flag, *any* red flag that would tell her he was lying.

His cheek jumping.

Insincerity in his eyes.

But she saw nothing but warmth.

He traced the scar that ran from her nose to her ear with his index finger, and she shivered. Then he leaned over and softly pressed his lips against hers. She kissed him back, tasting wine on his tongue. He pulled her closer to him, and his kisses became harder. She felt a sexual hunger she couldn't remember feeling before. The more they kissed, the stronger it became.

"Do you want to go to your bedroom?" he asked, his voice breathy.

They were moving fast, too fast. But she didn't want to stop. "Yes," she whispered.

"You sure?" he breathed. "Because we can, you know, stop."

"I don't want to—"

He hastily scooped her up and carried her to the bedroom. He set her down on the bed and slipped her shirt off, then unclasped her bra. He trailed his fingers slowly up her ribs, his fingers on her skin hot and electric. She moaned as he molded one of her breasts with his hand and took the other one into his warm mouth. She fumbled to unbutton his jeans and lower his zipper and listened to his breathing grow louder.

From there, everything became a blur of lips, hands, and skin. Their bodies one, the outside world melted away. All her worries had been silenced.

When they were done, he wrapped an arm around her and nuzzled her neck. "My God. You have no idea how long I've wanted to do this, Chelsea," he whispered. "No idea."

CHAPTER 9

LANG HAD TAKEN up temporary residence at a motel in Southie. He sat on a chair next to one of the two full-size beds, sipping a stale coffee he'd bought at the convenience store around the corner. Scattered across the bed were various files, photographs, and police reports.

He thought of what Chelsea had said about just happening to run into Boyd Lawson at the farmers' market. He remembered Lawson well. When he'd interviewed him after the killings, the kid had been a drug user—prescription pain pills, mostly—and he'd been tight-lipped. Possibly because he knew something that he wasn't sharing? Or maybe he was nervous he'd get implicated and they'd find out more about his drug use? Lang hadn't been in charge of the investigation long enough to find out.

He wondered now about their chance run-in with each other. Had it really been by accident? And just what did *reconnecting* mean? Was it just a friendship? Or something more? He found himself personally hoping it was simply a friendship. He'd developed a soft spot for Chelsea over the years and knew she could do much better.

The wood-paneled walls and heavy maroon drapes kept out all ambient light, so it seemed much later than it was, which made him feel sleepier than usual. He had replaced the generic artwork that adorned two of the room's walls with crime photos and news articles. The soft glow from the lamps mounted above the room's two nightstand tables gave him barely adequate reading light. But it was all he needed.

Garcia's call had sparked something in him. Over the years, the Springfield Coed Killings had bothered him. Now he had a chance to approach the case with a new vigor, affording him a sense of purpose he hadn't enjoyed in years, ever since the accident that had truncated his career. He wished he could confer with Detective Duplechaine, because his case files were extraordinarily messy. But Duplechaine had died of a heart attack while on the job a year earlier, so that wasn't a possibility.

Although it was likely that Ethan had been the one who had left the note on Chelsea's car, Lang decided that while Garcia and his team put out their APB—interviewing neighbors and local workers to see if they'd seen anyone in the area fitting Ethan's description—Lang would work the Springfield killings from ground zero to make sure they hadn't missed anything important.

He sipped his coffee as he shuffled through the crime photos and again found the note written on the mirror that night:

YOU MADE ME

The message had been etched in his brain long ago, along with all the questions that came with it.

Who was the note meant for? One of the victims? The police?

Was it a personal message to one of the two dead girls?

Was it a personal message to Chelsea?

Were the killings retribution for something?

In his first two days on the case, he'd looked for any other crimes that year or the two years preceding it that seemed to be related. He didn't find any. But that didn't mean there hadn't been one.

He picked up his phone, dragged his thumb across the screen, and called the Boston PD to see if the handwriting or fingerprint analyses had come back yet.

Garcia wasn't in, so he left a message.

He cracked his knuckles, then taped the photograph of the message left in the bathroom on the wall next to a photograph of the note Chelsea had received a few days ago. He stood back and studied both. Although there were slight variations, the handwriting was very similar.

But why would Ethan return after five years? What would he gain by toying with Chelsea and sending her an ominous note?

Was he worried she'd recovered memories from that night? And why now?

Did he perhaps get off on striking fear into her?

In people in general?

Or could it be just another part of the psychoses that had led him to kill in the first place?

He sat down and scribbled these questions in his notebook, then stood again and taped a large poster-size piece of paper to the wall. He wrote in big letters across the top: *Evidence.*

He glanced at the evidence report and wrote out a fresh list:

- *Fingerprints throughout house.*
- *Small traces of Ethan's DNA on Christine's body.*
- *Ethan's fingerprints on the knife block that housed the suspected weapon. Missing knife.*
- *Ethan's disappearance, along with his car, wallet, and government-issued identification.*

Lang hung another sheet of paper next to the evidence list. He drew a large question mark at the top of it, then started drafting a list below it:

- *Weapon never found.*
- *No sign of Ethan since killings.*
- *No activity of any kind after the killings: credit cards, phone calls.*

He studied the list for several minutes. Most killers inadvertently revealed themselves within the first forty-eight hours, when they were still high on adrenaline and not thinking straight. They might make a call, use a credit card to buy gas to get out of town, or do a hundred other things that would leave a trace. Ethan had done none of those things. He'd left no paper trail. Not even one photograph from a toll-road surveillance camera.

This behavior, to Lang, suggested that the killings might not have been crimes of passion or impulse but premeditated.

And with a very focused and disciplined planner.

But why?

What could the motive have been?

Lang wrote the word: *Motive.*

Chelsea's last memory, of growing tired and everything fading to black, had led Lang to initially believe the girls had been given Rohypnol, the best known of the so-called date-rape drugs. But toxicology reports for Rohypnol and other commonly used sex-assault drugs, like ketamine or GHB, all came back negative. That had been just one of the many dead ends in the investigation.

He pulled out photos of the victims' bodies. Studied them yet again. Tacked them up on the wall. Then he made a checklist of what he needed to do next.

He would speak with Ethan's mother, Michelle Klebold, again. Ethan's father, Charles, a successful investment banker in Manhattan, had died of a stroke a year after the killings. Charles had been shocked when Lang had first shown up at their house, asking about Ethan's whereabouts. A later report, from Duplechaine, showed that Charles had become borderline hostile when Duplechaine questioned him about the possibility that Charles and Michelle could have helped Ethan flee the country. Michelle Klebold's behavior had been consistent throughout the investigation. She'd been morose and almost despondent, claiming to be worried about Ethan's whereabouts and welfare. She'd quickly become a recluse, not wanting to show her face anywhere.

Lang forced another sip of coffee, then winced. His back was flaring up again, but he didn't want to take his pain pills.

Not tonight.

He took them only when totally necessary. They made him too drowsy and his mind fuzzy, and he needed to stay sharp. He still had a lot of work to do before morning. It was going to be a long night.

He got up and went to the kitchenette, where he had unloaded the vitamins and protein powder Victoria had made him promise to take. He'd also promised Victoria he'd eat vegetables and drink plenty of water. And that he would call every night.

He opened the fridge and took out a carrot, peeled it with a knife over the sink, tossed it on a plate, and drizzled hot-wing sauce next to it. That would take care of his vegetable requirement.

Then he unscrewed the lid to the protein powder and pulled out one of the joints he'd rolled earlier—a pain medicine he had found to be as effective as many of the prescription pills his doctor had given him. He grabbed a lighter from a cabinet and then went outside. The night sky was gloomy. Another storm was rolling in. Boston had been getting hit with back-to-back storms over the last several months, while Springfield had remained dry. In fact, it was quickly turning into Springfield's driest year on record.

He rolled his thumb across the lighter's wheel, and the flame popped to life. He lit the joint, then snapped the lighter closed and took a long hit.

Although completely worn-out and in pain, he was happy that he was able to pick up this case. Had his supervisor known the true extent of his injuries, he never would have rehired him. Thankfully, upon early discussions about coming back to work on cold cases, Lang had found a physician who'd given him a much cleaner bill of health than his body could actually support. He couldn't allow his accident, his injuries, to hold him back anymore. He knew he could do the job. He would just have to pace himself.

The joint burning between his thumb and index finger, he took another hit and let his mind wander back to those few days he'd worked the case. He again remembered finding Chelsea Dutton. It was a scene that would be imprinted on his brain forever. He also recalled his visits to the parents of the deceased girls. Those were always the worst part of his job. The sky had still been gray a little after eight that morning when he'd knocked on the front door of Amy Harris's parents' house. Her mother had been in flannel pajamas when she'd answered the door, her auburn hair disheveled from sleep. Mr. Harris had walked up behind his wife, and they had hesitantly invited him in, obviously fearing the worst. Lang broke the news the best way he knew how, told them that their daughter had been found dead. Mr. Harris had turned white as a sheet. Mrs. Harris had promptly slapped Lang hard across the face, then fell to her knees on their hardwood floor and wailed at the top of her lungs. After all this time, their pain still lived inside him. He'd wanted for so long for them and the others involved to get their justice. Now he was getting his shot.

Don't screw it up, Lang.

He took another drag. A few minutes later, when his pain was down to a manageable level, he snuffed out the joint, opened the door to his motel room, and was greeted with a veil of heated air.

He stuck the joint back in the protein canister and was hanging the "Do Not Disturb" sign on the doorknob when his phone rang. He tossed the matches on the counter and grabbed it.

He looked at the screen. It was Victoria.

He swiped his thumb across the screen and brought the phone to his ear.

"Hi, doll."

"Hi, Pop. How's the case going?"

It was great to hear her voice. He missed her and Nicky.

They spent a couple of minutes talking about the case. About Nicky and how he was tolerating the extra three hours of day care in the afternoons since Lang wasn't there to help take care of him. Then he talked with Nicky, who asked if he'd bring him something when he got back. When Victoria returned to the phone, Lang could tell she wanted to say something but was hesitating.

"What is it, sweetheart?"

Silence.

"Victoria?"

"Are you going to be all right out there?"

"Of course. Why wouldn't I be?"

"Well, you've just been . . ."

"Been?"

"You've been drinking a lot lately, Pop."

Yes, he had, but he didn't think she'd noticed. He thought he'd hidden it better than that. Besides, it was a mistake. For months, he'd been becoming something he swore he'd never become: a cliché. The depressed cop who drank alone late at night. He hadn't been the type who staggered to bed every night. He'd been the type who did it quietly, secretively. The kind who had learned how to function while under the influence. But obviously he hadn't been as secretive as he'd thought. Victoria had noticed and been worried.

But he'd made some changes in the last few weeks. He'd slowed down significantly on the drinking. Had started supplementing the missed alcohol with the pot. Traded vodka for beer. Anything to avoid the pain pills most days and nights. He hated how they made him feel. Yes, he still had to take them, but usually no more than a couple of times a week.

He wouldn't tell her any of this, though. It was something he needed to work through alone.

"Pop?"

"Yeah. I'm here."

"I just worry. About you, the drinking. But I also know you need this. The case, I mean. Being on the job again. I know it's not enough for you to play Mr. Mom around the house anymore. I get it that you need more than that. But that doesn't mean I don't still worry about you."

"I'll be fine, Vic."

Silence.

Victoria hated to be dismissed. He could hear Nicky crying in the background.

"And Pop?"

"Yeah."

"Janie told me she's been trying to reach you, but you're not returning her calls."

Janie.

"You shouldn't avoid her. She loves you. And she's a great lady."

Victoria didn't get it. Of course he knew Janie was a great lady, which was exactly why he *wasn't* responding. He'd told Janie that it would be best to just be casual. That he wouldn't mind if she dated other men. It had hurt him to tell her that, but he'd needed to be fair to her.

After he hung up, he twisted open a beer, enjoying the cold maltiness on his tongue, its smoothness as it slid down his throat. But not so much the pang of guilt for having worried Victoria. She and Nicky were his heart. They were everything to him.

He went back to the bed and regarded the files before him. He was going to go through everything as many times as it took, until he got to the bottom of this.

He wasn't going to let the killer slip through his fingers again. He was going to solve this thing. Once and for all. He wasn't leaving Boston until he did.

CHAPTER 10

CHELSEA'S EYES FLUTTERED open to crisp sunlight pouring into her bedroom. Her heart swelled in her chest, remembering last night. How great it had felt to be intimate with Boyd, both physically and emotionally. She rolled over to face him.

And found his side of the bed empty.

She blinked, feeling a stab of disappointment. Had he left during the night without saying goodbye?

She sat up and instantly felt the dull throb of a headache. She rubbed the back of her head, regretting the amount of wine she'd drunk last night.

Then she saw something on her nightstand.

A note.

She grabbed it and lay back against her pillow. She unfolded it and blinked a few times until the letters came into focus.

Chelsea, I have an early-morning meeting at one of my shops, but you looked so incredibly peaceful, I couldn't bear to wake you. YOU are amazing in every way. I'll text you later. Love, Boyd

Love?

A memory flashed in her head.

Last night.

He'd whispered in her ear: *I think I fell in love with you the first time I laid eyes on you.*

Her heart galloped in her chest.

Had he really said that? Or had her drunken mind manufactured it? *Surely, he hadn't . . . didn't . . .*

Maybe she'd just dreamed it. After all, it would be very odd for him to say something like that when they'd been intimate for such a short time.

Her face stung from where the sharp stubble on his face had scraped her skin. As she slid out of bed, she felt a rawness between her thighs from—

Her smile widened as she remembered.

It had been a great night.

Better than great.

She made her way into the bathroom and stood beneath the showerhead, letting the hot water rush over her body. As the pounding water slowly revived her brain, she found herself curious about Boyd's early-morning meeting. He hadn't mentioned it last night, not that it meant anything. There were a lot of things about her days that she never mentioned to anyone.

She turned toward the spray and let it roar down against her forehead, then the top of her scalp—and forced the thought from her mind. There was absolutely no reason to suspect Boyd of lying, so she wouldn't. She hated that her mind always seemed to go to the worst place possible.

Focus on last night.

Not just the sex, but the connectedness.

Think positive thoughts. Not paranoid ones.

A few minutes later, she sat on the balcony, drinking coffee and watching Harry attack his scratching pad. The morning air was freezing, and it felt and smelled fresher than usual, the way it always did after a heavy rain. She listened to the tinkling of a neighbor's wind chimes and watched passersby strolling up and down the sidewalks below . . . and tried her best not to try to spot Ethan.

She thought more about Boyd. About the fact that since reconnecting with him, she hadn't had the nightmare even once. And she was enjoying a lightness in her chest . . . was it *joy*? For the first time that she could even remember. Maybe she hadn't realized how lonely she'd been. Hadn't realized that while she was busy trying to protect herself, she'd mistakenly made her world too small.

She thought again of what Boyd (might have) whispered in her ear. *I fell in love with you the first time I laid eyes on you.*

Had he really said that? She wondered again. If so, it was much too fast. It could also indicate that he was just on the rebound.

A key turned in the door. Chelsea looked down at her watch: 8:00 a.m. Almost time for the farmers' market. The door opened, and Elizabeth appeared. She walked in and yawned, looking frazzled and exhausted.

Her nursing shoes squeaked across the Pergo as she made her way to the balcony and plopped down on a chair. She looked at Chelsea and grinned tiredly. "What's with the big smile on your face?"

Chelsea hesitated for a quick moment, but then she decided to tell Elizabeth everything.

CHAPTER 11

A WEEK LATER, the air outside felt heavy and charged. The streets bustled with Bostonians as Chelsea plunged her hands deep inside her pockets, her pepper spray at the ready, and walked briskly toward her car. They still hadn't found Ethan, and she was growing impatient.

Thunderclouds crowded the sky, promising yet another storm. The wind tossed leaves and an empty potato-chip bag in her path, but she concentrated on her surroundings. It was the first time she'd ventured outside alone since finding the note, and she felt a sense of unease.

The past week, she had been back to her normal routines with everything except her morning runs, which she really missed. She'd just worked her regular hours and spent most of her evenings binge-watching television shows by herself. Elizabeth had been working overtime at the hospital and spending a lot of time with a pregnant coworker of hers, so Chelsea had been on her own.

A block from her car, she spotted a blond man wearing sunglasses who matched Ethan's height and build. He was on the sidewalk, advancing quickly toward her. She felt a surge of panic and sprinted to the other side of the street, then ducked into a bakery.

When she looked back, he was almost two blocks away, still walking quickly.

It had just been another of her false alarms.

She spent the final block of her walk trying to calm down and talk herself out of her anxiety. When she was about fifty feet from her car, her breath caught again. Something was glistening on the sidewalk next to the passenger door.

What the . . . ?

When she reached her car, a cold flush swept over her skin. A large stone, the size of a softball, was on the hood, a sheet of paper was wrapped around it, secured with a rubber band, and her windshield had been shattered. She looked around, her eyes brimming with tears.

An old couple passed by her, staring curiously at her car, then at her. The woman's mouth moved as though she was saying something, but the blood pounding in Chelsea's ears was so loud, she couldn't hear her words.

Chelsea hesitantly reached for the stone. She unfastened the sheet of paper and peered at it. Vines of ice wound up her neck. Someone had written a message with red marker.

YOU'RE GOING TO MAKE ME DO IT AGAIN, AREN'T YOU?

❖ ❖ ❖

AN HOUR LATER, Detectives Lang and Garcia rose from the kitchen table to leave. Garcia had bagged the stone and taken Chelsea's statement. She was exhausted and wanted nothing more than just to crawl back into bed. Finding the second note and her windshield shattered was more than she could handle right now.

"I'll request a patrol to pass by the building once a day until we have more, but I can't make any guarantees," Garcia said. He was a husky man, Hispanic, much bigger than Lang, very matter-of-fact. He'd shown up in a wrinkled beige suit and Lang in street clothes and a blazer.

"Thanks, I'd appreciate that," she said. She folded her arms around her waist, willing herself not to shake.

Garcia smiled and went to the door. Garcia was nice enough, but he didn't inspire the trust that Lang did. But then again, she and Lang had a history.

"Again, be vigilant. Try to always be with someone when you go out," Lang said. "Especially at night."

"Okay."

"And your job. You're still able to do it here, from your apartment, correct?"

"Yes, sir."

"Okay, good. So, then, I take it there's no reason for you to go out after dark?"

"No, sir."

As she walked them out, Lang turned to her. "You look exhausted. Maybe get some rest? I'll call and check up on you later."

❖❖❖

TWO HOURS LATER, Chelsea sat on the couch, aimlessly flipping through the channels while Elizabeth paced from the kitchen to the living room and back, holding a magazine she'd brought with her. She'd ripped out three pages and tossed them on the coffee table. All pictures of hair cut into angular-style bobs.

With the help of two Valium, Chelsea was now relatively calm.

But Elizabeth was not.

Elizabeth kept ticking off pages of her magazine. Her features were harder than usual, her brows meeting in the middle. The vein in her forehead was more pronounced, the way it became when she was angry and had something to say. Chelsea knew that whatever it was, Elizabeth was biding her time before saying it.

Over the years, she had learned to leave Elizabeth alone when she got like this. It didn't happen often—her being angry—but when she was, Chelsea made sure to stay out of her way because negative energy had a way of seeping into her blood and making her want to leap out of her skin.

She understood Elizabeth's anger. Her serious issues with disrespect, bullying, really with any injustice. And Elizabeth was very protective of her, so she was angry now because Chelsea was being screwed around with.

Chelsea also thought Elizabeth tended to overreact a little. Whether it was with a company who had double charged one of them for a product or demanding that the apartment manager immediately fix a leak or faulty toilet, sometimes Elizabeth could get pretty unhinged fairly quickly. Once in a while, she'd get so worked up, she'd go on antiestablishment rants. About how she didn't trust the country's banking system, the corruption of its politicians, corporations, and government agencies. In a way, Chelsea understood it. Elizabeth, like herself, had spent some time in the foster system, which wasn't Disneyland for any kid. And although Elizabeth had never gone into detail about her experiences, Chelsea knew enough to know that she had suffered abuse while she was there, and that the abuse had created a woman with many sharp edges.

But thankfully, only when she was provoked.

Chelsea watched Elizabeth continue to flick the pages of the magazine, flipping way too fast to be really looking at anything. Then finally, she tossed the magazine on the coffee table and sighed. "So, I take it that things have become serious between you and Boyd?"

Chelsea decided to tread lightly, knowing Elizabeth was bringing up Boyd because she thought he had something to do with the notes. After all, she'd mentioned it before. And could Chelsea blame her? She had struggled with her own suspicions. She was fully aware of how it looked. Boyd showing up out of nowhere the exact same time the notes began to appear. But the better Chelsea got to know Boyd, the more ridiculous the idea was that he could do something like that. He just wasn't the type.

"I don't know about serious, but things are good."

"Do you trust him?" Elizabeth asked.

Chelsea shrugged. "Yeah. I do trust him. To an extent, of course."

"Not completely?"

Of course she didn't trust him completely. But that wasn't a reflection on Boyd. She didn't trust *anyone* completely. Elizabeth was as close as anyone got.

Chelsea decided to just come out and acknowledge what Elizabeth was thinking. "If you're asking if I think he's the one leaving the notes, then no. It's Ethan."

Elizabeth regarded her for a long moment, then exhaled loudly. "I agree. It probably *is* Ethan. But listen to me for a moment, okay?"

"Okay."

"Look, I want more than anything to just be supportive of your relationship with Boyd. I want to be supportive because I see the changes in you. You're happier than I've ever seen you. Way happier." Her eyebrows furrowed. "But don't you think it's awfully suspicious that right after you meet up with the guy again, all hell suddenly breaks loose with these notes? And not only that, but if the guy was so wounded by everything that happened in Springfield, like you said he is, wouldn't he want to stay away from you? Far away from *anything* that reminded him of the murders?"

"You would think so, but *I* didn't. Honestly, I think that's part of the attraction," Chelsea said. "That he *was* there that night. I know it sounds weird. But maybe you would have had to have been there to understand it. The best way I know to explain it is that he helps me feel more connected to the person I was before the attacks. The person I still can't fully remember. Maybe I miss that person."

Elizabeth studied her.

"Besides, Boyd had no clue a message had even been left on the mirror that night, so if he *was* the one leaving the messages now, how would he even know what to write? It makes no sense."

Chelsea could hear Harry scratching at something in his little hideout beneath the couch.

"They were roommates, right?" Elizabeth asked. "Boyd and Ethan?"

"Yes."

"So, what if Boyd and Ethan are still in touch with each other? What if they're in on this note business together? I'm not saying they are, but what if? Seriously, these are questions you need to ask yourself."

Chelsea felt herself bristle. She didn't like where this conversation was going. And she could feel a headache coming on. "Boyd wouldn't do that," she said, looking past Elizabeth. She was tired of seeing the doubt in her eyes.

"I'm worried is all. Just promise to be careful with him, okay?"

Chelsea nodded.

"Okay. So, now that that's out of the way," Elizabeth said, "I brought you something."

Chelsea watched Elizabeth reach down to the other side of the recliner and pick up her purse, then carefully pull out something wrapped in black oilcloth. She removed the cloth and revealed a handgun.

Chelsea's head pounded. Just looking at the weapon gave Chelsea the heebie-jeebies. For her, it represented violence, death.

"Just hear me out," Elizabeth said. "I spoke to this guy at the gun shop in Dorchester. He's an ex-cop and teaches self-defense classes. He recommended this one for you. He says women like it because it's small and can fit in a purse easily. I also worked out some shooting lessons at the gun range." Elizabeth held out the gun. "Just hold it. It won't hurt you. I promise."

Reluctantly, Chelsea took the weapon from Elizabeth's hands. It was surprisingly light, probably less than a pound.

"So, are you cool with taking the lessons?" Elizabeth asked.

"I guess so."

"Okay, good. Because there's something else."

"What?"

Elizabeth hesitated. "Look, I wasn't sure if I should tell you this, but I think I have to."

"What is it?"

"Don't freak out, but I think I might've seen Ethan last night."

CHAPTER 12

ELIZABETH WAS LATE. It was 5:30 a.m., and the sun was still below the horizon. Chelsea sat in her car, sipping hot coffee and staring at the single-story, redbrick building that housed the shooting range. It looked identical to all the other buildings in the industrial park except for the small sign on the door that read "Suffolk County Gun Club."

She thought about Elizabeth possibly seeing Ethan. Elizabeth said she'd seen someone of his description standing next to a sedan on Dartmouth, not far from where Chelsea thought she'd seen him in a car a couple of weeks earlier.

Chelsea looked at the building again. Although she didn't yet have a license to carry a handgun, Elizabeth knew the owner of the gun club, and he'd agreed to allow them inside before opening hours. The license would have to come a little later.

The front door to the building flew open, and a short, stocky man looked out. He looked to be in his early thirties, with longish black hair and a heavy five o'clock shadow. His eyes found her. He pointed to her and waved her to the door.

Crap. Where's Elizabeth?

Chelsea switched off the ignition and stepped out of the car.

"You Elizabeth?" he called.

"I'm her friend Chelsea. I'm afraid Elizabeth's late."

"You're the friend who wants to shoot?"

"Yeah."

"Okay, good. Curtis told me to expect you. Come on in. I'm Tony."

Inside, the two stood in what looked like a waiting area at a doctor's office, except the magazines were all copies of *Field & Stream* and the posters on the walls were all of rifles and hunting gear.

Tony walked behind the counter. "Can I see it?" he asked, holding out his hand.

Chelsea pulled the handgun out of her large tote, unwrapped it, and handed it to him. Tony studied it. He felt the weight, checked the magazine and the barrel.

"Ruger LC9. Good little pistol. Seven-round magazine. Nice firearm for protection."

Tony looked up at her. His eyes took in the scar on her cheek, but he didn't ask. He waved for her to follow him again, and they walked through a door into a long hallway with several offices off to either side. The place was empty, and the only light was a single fluorescent strip in the center of the hallway. Chelsea noticed an odor in the air. Sulfur. It reminded her of the odor after a fireworks display, maybe combined with oil.

They walked through another door and into another room. She recognized it instantly as a shooting range from what she had seen in movies and on TV. It was a long, narrow room separated by several felt-covered wooden panels into individual shooting cubicles. Even though the rest of the room was dark, she could see that the cubicles all opened out to an empty room about seventy-five yards deep.

Tony set her up in one of the cubicles and flipped a switch, illuminating a target about fifty yards in front of her. She had been expecting the target to be a human silhouette, but it was just a generic circular target. He handed her a pair of heavy, protective earmuffs and safety goggles, then reached in a bucket and grabbed another set of earmuffs and goggles for himself.

Tony loaded the magazine with bullets and took aim at the target. When he shot the gun, the loud pop was very different from the usual sound guns made in movies. Still, the fact that it was a real gun shooting real bullets made her mouth go dry.

After shooting twice more, Tony nodded in approval and handed the gun to Chelsea.

"You know how to hold it?"

"No. I don't know anything."

"No problem." He stood behind her and showed her how to hold the gun, how to aim it, and how to squeeze the trigger. She didn't like the way it felt in her hands. It felt wrong. The thought that someone could be killed with what was between her palms made her uncomfortable. But Elizabeth was right. With Ethan out there, she did need something in the apartment stronger than pepper spray. If someone tried to break in, it would be either her or him. And now with Boyd in her life, she was pretty sure she wanted to live.

Tony backed away so she could fire. She aimed and squeezed the trigger. It kicked, but not as bad as she thought it would. She looked over at Tony.

"Go ahead." He smiled.

She returned her attention to the target and fired again.

And again.

By the time the magazine was empty, she was feeling more relaxed, more accepting of the weapon. She set it down on the counter, realizing the barrel was warm to the touch.

Tony stepped forward and pressed a button. She heard a buzzing sound, and the target slid on an electric conveyor belt toward them. Most of her shots were in the circle. Two in the bull's-eye.

"Jesus, lady. You're a natural. You sure you never fired a gun before?"

Chelsea smiled at the compliment.

"Smoking hot *and* a sure shot. No wonder you need protection. I bet guys are climbing all over each other to get to you."

More like shattering windshields and leaving sinister notes.

She watched him yank the target off the conveyor. He handed it to her, then clipped on a fresh target and sent the conveyor back out.

"I don't think you need lessons, but I'd be happy to give you some, anyway. In exchange for, maybe, dinner with me sometime?" He lifted an eyebrow.

The phone in the front office rang. He groaned and rolled his eyes. "Jesus. The phone rings off the hook here. Feel free to fire some more. I'll be right back."

Left alone in the shooting range, Chelsea dug around in her purse for her phone to try Elizabeth again.

"Hey, how's it going?"

She spun around.

It was Elizabeth. "Sorry I'm late. But it's so damn early," she said, yawning. Elizabeth pointed to Chelsea's used target. "You do that?"

Chelsea nodded.

"No way."

"I'm serious." Chelsea smiled.

"Damn, girl!"

Chelsea shrugged. "I got lucky."

"Let's see you shoot some more. See if you have a sophomore slump."

Chelsea fumbled with the bullets but eventually loaded the magazine and clipped it into place. She pulled her ear gear and safety goggles on and told Elizabeth to do the same.

Her second round was just as good as the first. She pushed the button that pulled the target toward her. Elizabeth whistled when she saw the holes in the paper.

"So, what do you think?" Chelsea asked, proud of herself for her previously unknown skill.

"What do I think?" Elizabeth aid. "I *think* Ethan better watch his back."

The mention of Ethan's name brought Chelsea back to reality and the reason why she was firing a gun in the first place. She felt the smile on her lips fall a little.

"Look," Elizabeth said, "I know you aren't crazy about this, but you'll be glad you have it. If nothing else, it should bring you some peace of mind that it's there if you need it."

"You're right," Chelsea said. "Thanks for doing this for me. Going through all the trouble of getting the gun. Setting up the lessons. You're an awesome friend."

Chelsea heard a cough behind her. She turned to see Tony standing by the door that led to the offices. He was staring at her oddly.

"You okay?" he asked.

Chelsea nodded.

"Sure?" he asked. He looked concerned, or was that irritation? Maybe anger? She couldn't tell. Had he overheard their conversation? Heard her mention Ethan and maybe thought she was talking about a boyfriend? He had been flirting with her earlier. Had he thought he had a chance with her?

"Okay, then I'll be in the office up front," he said. "If you need anything, let me know. You have about thirty more minutes."

"Okay, thanks."

Chelsea turned back to Elizabeth, who was busy folding the used targets into fours. Elizabeth looked at her.

"You're welcome. I'm glad to see it didn't take you long to learn your way around a gun."

Chelsea grunted.

"Seriously. You're quite the sure shot."

Chelsea grinned. "Eh. So I've been told."

CHAPTER 13

WHEN BOYD ARRIVED hours later, he leaned in and kissed her softly on the lips, making her breath catch in her throat.

After he put his stuff down and got settled in, they went out for a late lunch. They picked a Thai restaurant around the corner and sat at a quiet table in the back, ate, and talked.

Chelsea learned that he enjoyed a clean, tidy space just as much as she did. That he had a fear of small dogs (this one surprised her). That he was looking for a new job. Right now he was still working for his soon-to-be-ex father-in-law's company. He'd been doing a lot of soul-searching, trying to figure out what he would be passionate doing for the rest of his life. He said he still had no clue what he wanted to do, but he doubted it would be anything in sales. He talked a lot about his life, much more than he had before, and Chelsea got the feeling that a lot of what he was telling her had been bottled up for some time.

A couple of times during the conversation, she'd started to tell him about her windshield, but they were talking about mostly normal things, so she decided to wait until later.

As they ate dessert, he turned the conversation back to her. "Is there something you really want, but sometimes fear you'll never get?" he asked.

Yes, a lot of things. She thought for a moment. "Acceptance."

"What? Who wouldn't accept you?"

"Ha! I'd imagine a lot of people. Guys, especially." She motioned to her face, her arms, her hands. "Look at my scars. C'mon, you have to realize that not everyone has a scar fetish like you."

"No?" he asked, then winked.

She smirked. "Normalcy."

"Normalcy," he repeated. "That's a good one. But I wonder if anyone feels completely normal."

She thought about that. "That's a good point. I guess I've never thought about it that way."

He rubbed the top of her hand with his thumb. "Another one: What do you love?"

She looked up at the ceiling, trying to think. "Harry. Coffee. A clean apartment. The scent of lavender. Warm laundry. How about you?" she asked.

"Hmm. When the heater in the car starts actually blowing warm air."

She smiled. "Yeah, I like that one, too."

"You again," he said.

"Honesty. I also love honesty."

His eyes flitted to his empty plate. He looked back up at her and grinned. "Yeah. Honesty is good."

She noticed the hesitation and wondered what it had been about. Before she could ask, the waiter brought the check, and the moment was gone.

After lunch, they decided to take in a matinee. As she watched the movie on the screen, Boyd placed a hand on her upper thigh. Every once in a while, he gave it a little squeeze, sending shivers shooting through her body. And she realized she loved every second she spent with him.

Just a couple of weeks ago, her world had consisted mainly of her cat and Elizabeth. She'd been merely existing. Not living. Then in a blink of an eye, Boyd's presence had changed everything.

Five minutes before the movie ended, Boyd's breath was warm against her ear. "I brought my toothbrush. In case, you know, you want some company tonight."

Chelsea smiled in the darkness of the theater and felt a twinge in her middle.

Of course she did.

In fact, she wanted nothing more than to be with him.

After the movie, they went back to her apartment, and Chelsea let herself drink wine again. She had learned that she loved the numbness she felt after drinking a glass or two. It was pleasant, the polar opposite of the horrible, debilitating kind of numbness she'd suffered during her depressions.

They sat, drinking and listening to throwbacks like the Cure, the Smiths, even the Beatles. They talked more about their hopes and dreams. She was glad to see that the damage he'd suffered hadn't made his heart unkind. If anything, it just made him more sensitive to hurting others.

Two hours after they'd returned to the apartment, they were in bed. They had sex twice. The first time was hard and passionate. The next was softer, more sensitive. Later, they lay exhausted and content on her bed, watching a movie. The only time either of them got up was when Boyd answered the door for the pizza. While he was eating, she went to take a shower.

A few minutes later, as the hot water poured down over her face and body, she smiled, realizing she felt content and alive.

Actually happy.

She tried to commit the way it felt to memory, because she never wanted to forget it. She wanted this to last a long time.

Forever, if possible.

But as positive as she wanted to be about this new relationship, she was also realistic. No relationship was happy all the time. They took work. And most wouldn't stand the test of time. Everything was temporary, especially relationships.

She was so caught up in her thoughts, she barely heard the shower door open and Boyd step in behind her. She turned toward him and folded her arms around his neck, pressing her soapy body against him.

"I couldn't bear the thought of you in here naked and all alone," he murmured.

CHAPTER 14

CHELSEA AND BOYD slept in until 10:00 a.m. and were about to head out for breakfast when there was a knock on the door. Chelsea looked through the peephole and saw Lang. Her heart sped up at the possibility he might have new information.

"It's Lang," she told Boyd, who was on the couch pulling his shoes on.

"Who?" she heard him ask from behind her as she swung the door open.

"Good morning," she said to a tired-looking Lang. The man smiled, his eyes crinkling at the edges.

"Good morning. Have a couple of minutes?" he asked.

"Absolutely. Come in."

She moved aside so he could walk past her.

"I guess you two already know each other," she said, looking from Lang to a surprised-looking Boyd.

"Mr. Lawson." Lang nodded. "What a nice surprise."

Boyd stood up. "Detective Lang."

The two men shook hands.

"Want coffee?" she asked Lang.

"Sure. If it's not too much trouble."

She motioned for Lang to have a seat at her little kitchen table. "Is there anything new?" she asked, grabbing a bag of coffee grounds.

"Nothing to report on quite yet. I just came by as a courtesy call," he said from behind her. She heard him grunt as he sat down at the table. "Wanted to check in on you. Make sure you're doing okay."

Chelsea dumped coffee grounds into the pot's filter and filled the reservoir with water.

"I don't understand," Boyd said, still looking confused. "Are you living in Boston now?"

"No. I'm still in Springfield."

Chelsea realized she hadn't told him about Lang actively looking into the case again or about the rock and the message that had been written on it.

She turned to face them. "I received another note. And a big rock through my windshield."

"Wait. Are you serious?" Boyd asked.

"Yeah."

"When?"

She explained everything. When she finished, Boyd had a funny look on his face. One she couldn't place. "Why didn't you tell me?" he asked.

"I meant to. I just . . . I guess I just wanted to think of happier things for a little while. Then time kind of got past me."

Harry meowed and jumped up on Lang's lap, and the man pet him. "It's been a long time, Mr. Lawson. Chelsea told me you guys were back in touch."

Boyd nodded.

"So, how about you? Where are you living these days?" Lang asked.

"Marblehead."

"Marblehead? Good for you. That's a very nice area."

"Yeah."

"Affluent."

Boyd didn't respond.

"You drive here often?"

"Just when I have business here."

"Boston's a big town, so it's a bit of a coincidence," Lang said. "You and Chelsea, bumping into each other randomly like that. Especially with not even living here."

Boyd shrugged. "Happens."

"Yes, it appears so, doesn't it?"

Chelsea poured coffee for everyone.

"When did you guys reconnect?" Lang asked Boyd.

"A couple of weeks ago."

"Is that right?" Lang said. He took a small, leather-bound notebook from his jacket pocket.

"Two weeks ago. That was about the same time you received the first note, correct?" Lang's eyes flickered to Chelsea.

Boyd seemed to stiffen a little.

"Yes," Chelsea said reluctantly, handing Lang his coffee. She knew what he was thinking. It was bad enough that Elizabeth was already suspicious of Boyd. She didn't want Lang suspicious of him, too.

"Interesting timing," Lang said, peering up at her. His gaze swung back to Boyd. "So, have you heard from Ethan at all? Since the killings?"

Boyd frowned. "Of course not."

"Nothing? At all?" Lang asked.

"Nothing."

"Any knowledge of his whereabouts?"

Boyd shifted in his chair. "None."

Lang nodded and scribbled something down.

"You receive any strange notes like Chelsea has? Anything like that?"

Boyd shook his head. "Nothing that couldn't be explained."

"What about strange calls? Get any of those?"

Chelsea noticed the tip of Boyd's nose and ears were pink. He passed his hand over his mouth, then shook his head again. "No. None."

"I'm sorry. Are you uncomfortable with these questions, Mr. Lawson?"

"Not at all. Why?"

"Because you *look* uncomfortable."

"Well, I'm not."

"I'm just trying to piece things together. I'm sure you can appreciate that. You of all people want to see Ethan, or *whoever* it is who is doing this to Chelsea, behind bars, right?"

"Of course."

"Since you and Chelsea *reconnected*, let's see, two weeks ago, how many times have you visited here?"

"I don't know, twice? Three times?"

"Three times," Chelsea confirmed, although all the hours of texting back and forth between his visits had certainly made it feel like it had been more.

"So, you were here, in town, the day the first note was left on Chelsea's car. Is that correct?"

Boyd's eyes flashed. "What are you trying to say? That you think I left that note?"

Lang acted confused. "No. Of course not. Why would you do something like that? I was simply making an observation."

"I would never do anything like that. Never have. Never will. And I didn't even know he'd left a second note and done that to her windshield. I had no clue."

"I'm sure you didn't." Lang studied Boyd for a long moment, then stood up. "Well, I'd better get going. I have a meeting with Garcia. Thank you for your time, Mr. Lawson. Miss Dutton, I'm glad to see you're doing okay." He tucked his notebook in his coat pocket, then looked pointedly at Boyd again. "I'll be in touch again soon. Maybe next time we can talk more extensively, and in private. How about I come to you next? In Marblehead?"

"Why? I've told you everything I know," Boyd said.

"Maybe. But in cases like these, new questions spring up all the time."

Chelsea saw Lang out and watched him limp down the hall. She closed and locked the door, then turned to see Boyd standing in the living room, facing her.

"What the hell was that?" he said. He ran his fingers through his thick hair. "Jesus!"

Chelsea took a step back. It was obvious that Lang had been leaning hard on him, but she hadn't seen Boyd angry before. He was usually so gentle and even-keeled.

"What the hell does he want from me?"

He walked over to the balcony and looked out.

"Everything's fine. He just had a few questions. Why are you so freaked out?" she asked.

"Oh, jeez. I don't know. Because I was just interrogated by a homicide detective in connection to a *murder* investigation . . . again. And he looked at me the exact same way he did back then. Like I was a total piece of shit. It's how *everyone* looked at me those days. Like some people *still* do."

He turned to her. "Chelsea, I wasn't kidding when I told you that those murders ruined my life. And until just now, I thought most of it, *especially* when it came to the police, was behind me."

He sank into the couch but then jumped up again as though he couldn't sit still. "Jesus. I don't need this," he said.

Chelsea's heart fluttered in her chest like a trapped bird. "But he wasn't accusing you of anything."

"Then why did he say he would stop by my house?"

"What's wrong with him stopping by your house and asking a few more questions? He's trying to find Ethan. That's a good thing, right?"

"Right," he said. He started walking back to the balcony again, then whirled around. "Why didn't you tell me about the windshield?"

"Like I said, I wanted to think of happier . . . more *normal* . . . things for a little while. It's not a big deal."

"No. That's a *very* big deal. Something that you should have told me . . . oh, I don't know . . . *right after it happened?*" He rubbed the back of his neck. "I don't want to, no, *I can't* be in the middle of all of this again. I just can't."

His phone vibrated. He dug it out of his pocket and looked at the screen. He shook his head again and stuck it back in his pocket.

"What's wrong?"

"Nothing." He threw his hands in the air. "*Everything.* Shit, I don't know."

She wished he'd calm down. She wrung her hands, not sure how to help him. She glanced at her watch. It wasn't even noon yet, but she knew how much he liked to drink. "You want a glass of wine?"

He nodded. "Yeah, sure."

She went into the kitchen and opened a bottle of wine. She brought the bottle and glasses to the coffee table. He poured wine for both of them.

She took her glass and sat on the edge of the recliner. She wanted to reach out to him. Touch him. Reassure him. But she could feel his negative energy from where she was and couldn't bear to get any closer to it.

He finished his glass, then grabbed the bottle of wine and poured himself more.

She watched him stare out the French doors for a while. When the sun slid behind a large cumulus cloud, darkening the room to a dusky gray, she reached out to turn on a lamp. When she looked up again, Boyd was bent forward on the couch, rubbing his thumbs over his cheekbones. His wineglass was on the coffee table. Empty again.

He suddenly jumped up. "I gotta go."

Go? But why? He'd been planning to stay the night again.

The room shimmered in front of her eyes. "Let's talk about this. Or *not* talk about this. But don't go."

"I have to. Something's come up."

Come up?

What, aside from Lang's visit?

She wanted to ask but felt it would only upset him more. She blinked tears away as she watched him grab his shoulder bag and gather a few things. When he was done, he pecked her on the cheek, then walked to the door.

"I'll call you," he said.

And five seconds later, he was gone.

❀ ❀ ❀

Hours later, Chelsea was still sitting on the couch, trying to make sense of everything that had happened. Harry rubbed up against her calf and meowed softly. She picked him up, grabbed her phone, and decided to text Boyd. Although she'd always waited for him to text her first, today was different.

She'd felt a shift in him.

A big one.

And it scared her.

I hope everything's OK.

She stared out the French doors as she waited for his reply. Darkness was falling fast. The sky was streaked with clouds, and the shadows were thickening. After a long few minutes and no response from Boyd, she set the phone down, grabbed her wineglass, and refilled it.

She needed to feel comfortably numb again.

To not feel.

She lifted the wineglass to her nose, taking in the wine's fruity scent. *Grapes, apples, roses.* She sipped, hoping it would take her back to earlier that day when they'd been enjoying each other.

Hearing someone in the hallway outside her door, she jumped up.

Had Boyd changed his mind?

She started for the door but then heard a key slip inside the lock. When Elizabeth appeared, she sighed.

"Wow. Glad to see you, too," Elizabeth said. "Why the long face?"

Chelsea went back to the kitchen. "Want a glass of wine?" she asked, picking up the bottle to pour herself more.

"Uh-oh. This can't be good. You don't drink."

Chelsea grabbed another wineglass and poured Elizabeth some.

"I'd ask how your date with Boyd went, but I think I have a pretty good idea."

"I don't want to talk about it," Chelsea said and plopped on the couch.

The two silently polished off the bottle of wine as they watched bad reality TV. Chelsea occasionally excused herself to go to the bathroom, so she could send Boyd texts in private. The more she drank, the more texts she sent. But he still wasn't responding.

Was he blaming her for Lang's visit? Because if he was, that wasn't fair. She'd had no control over that.

Or maybe he just couldn't get to his phone for some reason, or maybe his phone was dead . . . and he'd just text later. Even though she was well on her way to being drunk, or maybe already was, she knew it was best to stop texting him. She was pestering him, which was the last thing she wanted to do.

When Elizabeth left at 11:00 p.m., Chelsea stumbled to her bedroom and crawled into bed. The apartment seemed extra quiet, and she felt an emptiness in her chest that up until that afternoon Boyd had been filling so very well.

She tried to shake off the feeling, remind herself she was rushing to conclusions, probably making something out of absolutely nothing. Boyd had just been surprised by Lang's visit. It had just been too much for him . . . reminding him of how horrible things had been for him back at the time of the murders.

He probably needed time to process the conversation with Detective Lang. Put it in perspective and cool off. He'd be okay tomorrow, and things would hopefully return to normal.

CHAPTER 15

CLASSICAL MUSIC BLARED from the radio of Lang's 2006 Crown Victoria during his two-hour drive to Newport. With 215,000 miles on it, the vehicle was deteriorating quickly, but it was paid off, and he had no desire to make a monthly car payment. Besides, he took meticulous care of it, and it showed. The gray-cloth interior looked surprisingly clean—especially for cloth. No stains, no cigarette burns. And, thanks to lots of tender loving care, the engine still purred like a kitten.

He couldn't tell a Brahms concerto from a Schubert waltz, but that didn't matter to him. He still liked to listen to classical music while he drove. It helped him think.

The classical piece he was listening to came to a climactic conclusion and was immediately replaced with the deep, soothing voice of the evening DJ. Lang switched off the radio, and his thoughts circled back to the rock left on Chelsea's shattered windshield.

Stretching his eyes open as much as possible in an effort to stay awake, he picked up the plastic travel mug from its cup holder and took a long sip, trying to rid himself of the oxycodone hangover he had from last night. Unfortunately, the throbbing in his back had become so intense, he'd taken the medication two nights in a row, and it was slowing down his mind and his work.

He'd visited with Garcia at his station in Boston that morning and found out that the analysis showed that the handwriting on the mirror of the Springfield crime scene matched the first note left on Chelsea's windshield, so the likelihood that Ethan was the one who left it was high.

Garcia's APB hadn't turned up anything. Neither had canvassing the neighborhood. No one remembered seeing anyone who matched his description. The fingerprint analysis had come back with only Chelsea's fingerprints, so the perpetrator had likely used gloves. Also, Garcia had run Ethan's credit report again and looked for any arrest records, but there'd been no activity under his Social Security number at all for almost five years.

"Are you leaving these messages, Ethan?" he spoke aloud.

If so, where are you?

He tried the radio again. A piano concerto filled the air just as he pulled the car onto the exit ramp toward Newport. He had an appointment with Ethan's mother. After Ethan's father had passed away, he'd left their expansive oceanfront estate to her, which was where Lang was heading now. Among other things, he needed to find out if she had heard anything from Ethan over the past years.

He pulled onto the long, winding road that led to the Klebold home and saw the sprawling redbrick English manor in the distance. The lawn was flawless and landscaped with meticulous detail. Lang had the feeling it had never been walked on by anyone other than the gardener.

As he climbed out of the car, he cursed his back. Shutting the vehicle's door, he counted more than a dozen windows along the front of the three-story house and wondered if Mrs. Klebold lived there alone.

He walked up to the house. Knocking on the massive door, he couldn't help but think there would be plenty of places to hide someone in a house this big.

CHAPTER 16

BOYD'S SILENCE SAT on Chelsea's chest like lead. It had been a week since she'd heard from him. Was he not receiving her texts for some reason? She knew that was just wishful thinking.

Of course he was.

Which meant he was avoiding her.

Does that mean he's done with me? Even after everything he said? After telling me that he loved me? That he'd been in love with me for years?

Had they just been words to get her to sleep with him?

No. That didn't make sense.

He'd told her those things *after* they'd had sex.

What could possibly be the point of saying them if they'd only been a lie? Why even waste his breath? And if his silence was due to Lang's questions, why? She analyzed and reanalyzed everything that had happened until her head pounded.

She looked around. Her apartment was cold, silent . . . lonely. It was also becoming cluttered, even filthy, and stank of old food. The kitchen trash can was overloaded with empty chicken-pot-pie boxes, Hungry-Man frozen dinners, ripped-open macaroni-and-cheese boxes, empty aluminum containers of precooked spaghetti. She'd even eaten a whole double-fudge cake in one sitting. The sink, counters, and coffee table were packed with dirty dishes, and Harry's litter box desperately needed changing. It was so unlike her. All of it. She had never allowed her place to become untidy, much less filthy. But she felt zapped of energy and didn't care.

She'd clean everything up.

Tomorrow.

She'd been staring at her computer screen for the good part of an hour, trying to transcribe doctors' notes from office visits—work that was due soon—but she couldn't manage to get her fingers or brain to work.

If they wanted to fire her for turning her work in late, so be it. She had more than $8,000 in the fireproof safe she kept in her closet. She could live on that for a little while if she absolutely had to.

She pushed away from her desk in frustration, wanting desperately to feel better. Maybe she could go on a run. She hadn't run in over a week now, frightened that Ethan was out there somewhere.

But screw him.

She needed a release, or she'd go insane. Besides, it was daylight out. If he was out there waiting for her, she'd be able to see him before he got too close. And people were already milling about, so even if he was out there, it wasn't very likely he'd try anything.

Seizing on the distraction, she went to her bedroom and shrugged on some running clothes. Then outside, she started off on her usual route, trying to ignore all the ghoulish Halloween decorations that had suddenly popped up on people's balconies, in storefronts, even at the public park: witches, ghosts, goblins, zombies, vampires, RIP signs, masks like Jason Voorhees wore in the *Friday the 13th* horror movies. Halloween was in less than a week. Just thinking of people celebrating death made her nauseated. It was so macabre. How could anyone think it was okay to glamorize death and murder? What a shitty thing to do.

Scanning her surroundings, she listened to her sneakers pound the pavement and took in chilly air laced with wood smoke and vehicle exhaust. Although daylight, it was still only a little after 7:00 a.m., so not many people were out yet.

Half a mile into her run, her nose flooded with the scents of whiskey and cigarette smoke, and the god-awful, excruciating memory of being curled up in the bathtub flashed in her head.

The white-hot pain.

The confusion, the fear.

Tears sprang to her eyes, and her legs began to feel heavy, leaden. She wiped at her eyes and nose with the heel of her hand and tried to breathe through her mouth. But the flashes kept coming, and she struggled to catch her breath.

Realizing running today wasn't going to happen, she turned and headed back. On the way, she decided to stop in at Owen's, a coffee shop two blocks from her apartment. An extra jolt of caffeine would do her good, and truth be told, she wasn't quite ready to return to the reality of her filthy apartment yet.

As she pulled the door open, she was immediately enveloped in the rich, familiar aroma of coffee. It should have been a comforting scent, but it wasn't. She was too wound up, too anxious. There was only a trickle of people inside the coffee shop. Just a few early-morning risers like herself.

Owen's was an older coffee shop. The kind of place the national chains worked so hard to emulate. Open-loft design with exposed pipes on the ceiling and hardwood floors. The furniture seemed to have been gathered from various thrift stores and garage sales, but it all fit together perfectly in a charming, pleasing kind of way.

As she waited for her turn to order, she watched an employee arrange homemade pastries and snacks on the shelves: cheese Danish, freshly baked cake loaves, a pan of chocolate brownies, and gingersnap cookies in the shape of cartoon ghosts.

She ordered a latte and a bottle of water and grabbed a corner seat near the window, where she knew it was unlikely she'd be bothered. She tried to focus on the melody of the acoustic guitar that drifted softly through the store's speakers, interrupted occasionally by the hiss of the espresso machine, and gulped the water down quickly to douse her dry throat. When she finished the water, she sipped her latte, stared out the window, and watched the city come to life.

It wasn't long before more people began to emerge from their apartments, filling the sidewalks outside. As the number of cars and pedestrians increased, she found her eyes darting back and forth through the crowds a little too much.

She was searching.

Like she always did.

As a large group of college kids trudged their way down the sidewalk, she caught a glimpse of someone in the distance. Someone who wasn't moving with the crowd. He was wearing a black skullcap, a matching leather coat, and a pair of sunglasses and was standing motionless on the other side of the street. He seemed to be staring at the coffee shop. Maybe even through the window at her.

The hair rose on the back of her neck.

Is that . . . Ethan?

She couldn't tell.

The espresso machine hissed again, making her jump.

"Excuse me, ma'am?"

She jumped again, this time almost dropping her cup of coffee.

She spun around and found herself staring into the face of a man. He was about forty and wearing a heavy red jacket.

He held out his hands. "I'm sorry. I didn't mean to scare you. I just wanted to ask if I could grab this chair?" He pointed to the chair across from her, then to a table where three other men were seated. They were one chair short.

Oh, God. I'm such a head case.

She was truly beginning to hate her own mind.

She managed a tight smile, although tears were pricking her eyes. "Yeah, sure."

As the man carried the chair over to his table, she dragged her gaze back to where she'd seen the guy across the street.

But the sidewalk was empty.

❈ ❈ ❈

That night, she lay on the floor of her living room, staring at the ceiling. Music whispered from the portable speaker connected to her phone. It was a Spotify playlist: Songs for the Brokenhearted. She wallowed in the melancholy music, sitting up every once in a while to take a bite of macaroni and cheese and wash it down with red wine from a bottle she'd wrestled open at noon.

She was having a pity party.

She knew that.

And she was aware that she was being ridiculous.

This must be what it feels like to be a young girl when your boyfriend breaks up with you, she thought. Except she was no longer a young girl.

Yes, she knew she'd been seeing him for a short time—okay, a *very* short time—but her connection to him had grown so deep so quickly. He'd filled a void that she didn't know she'd had. And now that he was gone, she was more painfully aware of it than ever. She ached with a loneliness she had never felt before.

She grabbed her phone and checked for texts, as though one would just magically appear. How could he just ignore her like this, with no explanation at all? Despite her good intentions, she typed a message:

Where did you go?

She pressed "Send" before she could talk herself out of it. Then she struggled to her feet and stumbled to her desk, placing one hand on the back of the couch for balance. She plopped down at her desk and opened her laptop. She needed to see him again, dammit. Even if it was just pictures.

She Googled *Boyd Lawson* and saw that there was a Boyd Lawson who was a bishop for Catholic Churches International.

No, not him.

She scrolled and clicked through ten pages of Boyd Lawsons. There was a profile for a Boyd Lawson on Facebook. But he lived in New Mexico. *Not him, either.* She clicked on the "Images" tab. More than two hundred photos appeared on her screen. Photos of white men, black men, group photos with men and women, photos of children. Not one of whom was her Boyd Lawson. She tried to remember the name of the car-detailing business he worked for but couldn't.

She Googled *car-detailing Marblehead*, and nine businesses popped up. She recognized the sixth one as Boyd's: Fine Brush. She clicked on the results and brought up a Yelp page with customer reviews. She pulled up Google again and went to the company's website and clicked on the "About Us" tab. A page appeared on the screen that declared they were a family-owned business. She scrolled and found him listed as the head of business development. Next to a short bio was a smiling Boyd. And next to him were two other bios. Fine Brush's owners: an older man with gray hair and a stunning blonde woman. The woman's name was Lisa Lawson.

His estranged wife, Lisa.

Her pulse racing, she went to Facebook and typed in *Lisa Lawson Marblehead.*

Bingo.

The same woman. Her relationship status said *married.*

She felt a crawl of horror in her stomach.

Married?

According to Boyd, they'd been estranged for almost a year, and the divorce was about to be final. Had that been a lie? Or had Lisa just not gotten around to changing her relationship status? Was Lisa hopeful that they'd work things out before the divorce became final, so she hadn't changed her status yet?

She expanded the size of Lisa's profile photo and studied it. The woman's beauty irritated her. She was gorgeous. Sleek blonde hair, beautiful blue eyes, and a perfectly straight nose. Full lips. Slender body, curvy in all the right places. Smooth, *unbutchered* skin.

Tears filled her eyes. Did Boyd still love her? He'd told her he didn't. That he'd fallen out of love a long time ago. Had he been lying? Had he been lying about them being estranged?

No. That isn't possible.

I'd know . . . right?

She clicked on Lisa's photo tab and found twelve large photo albums. Her hand trembling, she picked one that was labeled "Family" and slowly clicked through the photos: her wedding day with Boyd, at parties, skiing at some snow-covered destination, at restaurants with friends, on some lake. In every one of them, Boyd looked genuinely happy.

Had he only been acting as though he'd been happy with Lisa?

Or had he been acting with *her*?

She clicked back to Lisa's page and scrolled down her wall. The woman posted mostly real-estate listings, announcements about new restaurants and local businesses. She scrolled through six months' worth of status updates before slamming her laptop shut.

How could she be so stupid to open herself up to pain again when she'd been so hell-bent on protecting herself? Anger flaring in her belly, she stumbled into the kitchen and poured another glass of wine.

She was feeling sorry for herself, acting the victim, although she'd vowed never to do that again. She didn't do things like this. She was a fighter. A survivor.

Or was she?

She was starting to wonder.

A few minutes later, she made her way to her bedroom. She crawled into bed and closed her eyes. Listening to a moaning wind outside, she cried.

❀❀❀

The next afternoon, Chelsea awoke to thoughts of Lisa Lawson again. Of her relationship status declaring she was married. Then she looked around at her mess of an apartment, which had gotten even worse.

For the last several hours, she'd done little else than sleep and go to the bathroom. At one point, she had sliced open a bag of food for Harry, turned it on its side, and filled a big bowl of water for him.

She looked at the pile of untouched transcription work on the coffee table. A half-empty bottle of wine sat on top of it, next to a half-full wineglass.

A pathetic scene if she ever saw one.

And the fact that she'd mixed Valium with alcohol . . .

Not smart at all.

Dummy, dummy, dummy.

She felt a fresh rush of anger at Boyd for possibly not being estranged, for possibly still being very married. But then she turned her anger on herself. At the way she was handling it all. The way she was letting him get to her. The way she was behaving wasn't Boyd's problem; it was hers.

Get it together, Chelsea.

Stop this.

Now.

Why was she acting like this? She'd been so undisciplined lately. So irresponsible with her health. With her work. With her life. With her heart.

She'd been so taken with Boyd that she'd ignored everything else. She'd become completely unhinged because of someone who had reappeared in her life just a few weeks ago. Someone she'd hardly even known before. Even in her self-pity, she knew how absurd that was.

She peeled off her clothes, showered for the first time in days, then dressed in clean pajamas, determined to clean the apartment and get some work done. But when she walked back into the living room and surveyed the mess, she felt overwhelmed. Her renewed resolve fled her body, and she began to spin emotionally again.

She climbed on the couch and covered up. Harry pounced on her stomach and purred as though he knew she was struggling. "I love you, too, Harry," she whispered. She stroked his soft fur, glad to have something with a heartbeat to connect with.

She heard a key in the door.

Elizabeth.

She stiffened and buried herself deeper beneath her covers. Elizabeth had picked up more extra shifts at the hospital and hadn't been around for a few days, and Chelsea hadn't expected her today, either.

She heard the door open, then Elizabeth whisper, "Oh, my God."

Harry shot off the couch in pursuit of someplace to hide.

She listened to Elizabeth's shoes squeak as she walked around the room. She was looking at the mess. From beneath the covers, tears welled up in Chelsea's eyes. She clenched her fists so hard, her fingernails bit into her palms.

Go away. Please.

Leave me alone for a little while. I need to be—

"Jesus, Chelsea. Did you have a party and not invite me?"

Chelsea didn't answer her.

The couch protested as Elizabeth sat down. "Chelsea? Seriously. Are you okay? This mess. It isn't like you. My God, what happened? Stop hiding and talk to me."

Chelsea reluctantly emerged from beneath the covers, her cheeks soaked. She wiped at the tears with the heel of her hand.

"I'm an idiot is what happened."

Elizabeth frowned. "That's not true, and you know it."

"I'm *acting* like an idiot."

"This is about Boyd, isn't it?"

Chelsea nodded.

Elizabeth got up and turned on a lamp, then sat back down again. "What did he do?"

Chelsea told Elizabeth everything. About Lang's visit and how Boyd seemed to freak out afterward. Then how he'd abruptly left and was ignoring her texts.

"And he didn't give you an explanation?"

Chelsea shook her head.

"No anything?" Elizabeth asked.

"Nothing." Chelsea looked at her friend. "This is where you tell me, 'I told you so.' Because you did."

"Come on. I wouldn't do that." Elizabeth reached out and squeezed her shoulder. "I wish I'd been wrong. I'm sorry."

"And now . . ." Chelsea laughed. "I'm acting like a jilted teenager."

Elizabeth raised an eyebrow. "A teenager who can buy alcohol, I see."

Chelsea explained what she'd seen on Facebook. Lisa's relationship status indicating she was married.

Elizabeth's cheeks reddened. "What a sleazeball. I'm so sorry."

"Yeah, me, too." Chelsea shook her head. "What the hell happened to me? Why did I give him so much power? I thought I was stronger than this."

"You've been through a lot of shit, Chels. Of course you're going to have poor judgment sometimes. It just goes with the territory. But now that you've accepted that you were wrong about him, you can start getting over him."

"Yeah." Tears burned her eyes again, but Chelsea kept them at bay.

They talked a little more. When Elizabeth finally left, Chelsea was just about to take more Valium and slip into bed when a text came through.

She slowly picked up her phone. When she saw Boyd's name, her heart skipped a beat.

> Hey, sorry for being a stranger. Business has just been insane lately. I won't be back in the city for a few weeks, but when I am, maybe we can grab lunch.

She stared at the text. Read and reread it a dozen times. The first thing she noticed was that it lacked intimacy. The second was that Boyd was lying. Even *she* knew that if a man was interested in a woman, he always made time for her. Boyd was feeding her bullshit.

He was done with her, but he wanted to let her down easy. Her whole body shook as she read it one last time. Then she wrapped her arms tightly around herself and headed for the kitchen for something to crowd out the pain.

Midway there, she froze. An idea had popped into her head.

A crazy one.

Something she could do that might get her some answers. It wasn't something she'd normally do, but she was going to do it, anyway.

She hurried to her bedroom to get dressed.

CHAPTER 17

IN HIS MOTEL room, Lang continued to pore over the files.

He'd visited the parents of both deceased girls again and unfortunately learned nothing new. The only forward movement was that the second analysis had finally come back, and all the handwriting matched: the writing on the mirror, the note left on Chelsea's car, and the note left wrapped around the rock.

He pulled out his notebook from the piles of paperwork scattered across the bed. It contained thoughts he had written down during his interview with Ethan's mother. She had been very withdrawn. Having lost her husband, she seemed resigned to live out her life in solitude and maybe a little gin. It was one of the first things he'd noticed when she'd opened the door. An almost overpowering scent of alcohol wafting from her breath.

She'd told Lang that she hadn't seen or heard from her son since a week before the killings. And Lang couldn't help but believe her. He'd detected no nervousness. No deceit. Just resignation.

He finished off the microwaved hamburger he had picked up at a gas station. It was dry and tasteless, but it would have to do. He washed it down with another sip of coffee, then regarded the vitamins he'd promised Victoria he would take.

He glanced at his watch. It was getting late, and soon Nicky would be in bed. If he was going to call Victoria, he'd need to do it now. He sorted through the supplements and quickly downed them all because he knew Victoria would ask, and he didn't like to lie to her. Then he grabbed his phone and hit speed dial. Victoria answered on the first ring.

Sure enough, the first thing she asked was if he was taking his supplements. He assured her he was taking care of himself. She asked if there was any headway on the case, and he updated her on the little he knew. Then she asked the question he knew had been lingering in her mind the entire conversation.

"And Janie? Have you talked with her?"

"Victoria," he warned.

Silence.

As much as his daughter was pushing it, he couldn't let things with Janie progress. Not until he got his shit together. Of course, he cared about her. Hell, he maybe even loved her. Okay, not maybe. He *did* love her. What man wouldn't? Janie was not only attractive, smart, funny, and kind; she was also a self-made success. She'd built and sold a wellness blog for eight figures and never had to work again. So how the hell could he satisfy her? A washed-up former detective who relied on a small pension and supplementary cold cases to get by? Next to Janie, he hardly felt like a man sometimes.

He'd tried to explain that once to Victoria, but she hadn't agreed with him, which wasn't anything new. She thought Janie would love him regardless. Victoria was still young and idealistic.

"Pop?"

"I'm still here. But the topic of Janie is currently off-limits. Got it?"

He heard her sigh.

Ten minutes later, he hung up. His eyes went to the photograph of Boyd he'd pinned on the wall. Boyd had been very surprised to see him last week, and he'd definitely been nervous. Lang wondered if he was hiding something. But if so, what? He remembered Boyd from the day after the killings. He'd brought him to the station for questioning and found his alibi to be solid. He had been working at an all-night pizza shop when the slayings occurred, and he'd had a manager and surveillance video to vouch for him. Lang had wanted to spend more time with Boyd to learn more about Ethan, but his plans were interrupted by his car accident.

He needed to find out if Boyd was holding something back. He'd make an unannounced visit in Marblehead tomorrow morning. See if he could stumble upon something while he had the element of surprise on his side.

Listening to the steady dripping of the bathroom faucet, Lang lay on the floor and did the back stretches his physical therapist had recommended. He then went to the mini fridge and grabbed a beer and resumed his position on the side of the bed. He picked up a large manila folder stuffed with random notes and reports from Detective Duplechaine.

Duplechaine, unfortunately, had been incredibly disorganized and had written countless notes on scraps of paper he'd failed to have transcribed. Most were stuffed into big plastic baggies. Lang had already gone through the baggies once, but it was time to go through them again.

About twenty minutes later, he pulled out a stapled report, and a small Post-it note tumbled to the floor. He picked it up and read the words that had been scribbled on it in red marker next to a phone number:

Katherine—F/U immediately.

Katherine?

Who was Katherine?

The name didn't ring a bell. Frowning, Lang stood up and walked to the wall to see if anything jogged his memory, but he couldn't find anyone named Katherine.

Was she a friend of the girls? Of Ethan?

A witness?

There had been no reports filed about interviews with a Katherine. He'd gone through the file several times and was almost sure of it.

Then he had a thought. He searched through the papers scattered on the bed until he found the manila envelope he was looking for. Flipping through it, he found it—a list of Chelsea's foster-family members.

Lang read down the list.

Katherine Jones. She had been the daughter of John and Delores Jones. One of Chelsea's foster families.

Lang felt a twinge in his gut.

He grabbed his phone and dialed Katherine's number.

CHAPTER 18

IT WAS 9:00 p.m., and Chelsea was parked in an upper-middle-class neighborhood in Marblehead, four blocks from Lisa Lawson's house. She needed answers. If Boyd wouldn't give them to her, she'd have to get them herself.

The neighborhood was full of huge homes with expansive, well-manicured lawns, and just about every one of them was decorated for Halloween.

Lisa Lawson's house was a gorgeous two-story colonial with a horseshoe driveway made of brick and river rock. It angled off to a large four-car garage. It was one of the few houses that wasn't decorated for the ridiculous holiday. It also looked far too large for just one person.

It had taken all of five minutes to do an Internet search to find Lisa's home address. And Chelsea knew she had the right address when she spotted Boyd's Audi sedan in the driveway, along with another vehicle. An Audi SUV.

Tears immediately sprang to her eyes when she saw the two vehicles in the driveway, because it meant they were likely both home . . . together.

He had *lied, hadn't he?*

She climbed out of her car, pulled the hood of her coat so her face was mostly hidden, and walked toward the house. Her heart thundering in her chest, she debated knocking on the door. Asking Lisa . . . or Boyd . . . or *both of them* what was going on. It was time she found out. And once she did, she would go back to the way things were before. Go back to taking good care of herself. Go back to her old routines, the ones that had been working for her.

Something or someone else would happen for her when the time was right. Something just as good—no, *better* than Boyd.

If only she believed that.

She thought again about how she'd been struggling before Boyd had reappeared. How she'd felt as though she was just existing, and how depressing and hopeless that had felt. She forced the thought away.

The neighborhood was quiet at the late hour. Streetlights cast a soft glow over the meticulous front lawns. Porch lights highlighted beautiful brickwork on the faces of all the houses. She watched plumes of smoke curl out of chimneys, and she breathed it in through her nose. Even the air smelled better here than in the city. More expensive. The wood smoke a little sweeter.

Lights shone inside several of the homes, but she didn't see any of their inhabitants. She imagined this neighborhood didn't get a lot of people walking through at night. What would they think if they saw her? Would they call the police? She looked around, trying hard not to appear as though she was doing so, but saw no one looking out of the windows.

Her insides were jittery as she neared the house. The large front yard was landscaped with lush shrubbery, and golden mums lined the walk leading up to the front door. English ivy tumbled from ceramic planters on either side of the home's massive twin maple doors.

She walked past the house, crossed the street, and passed by yet again, trying not to be obvious but knowing she was probably violating a million stalking good practices. She should have thought of a plan of action before getting out of the car.

She passed the house one more time, craning her neck to get a look at the side windows. One on the first floor was lit. As she looked, she caught movement inside. A blur of beige or yellow.

Her pulse thudded in her throat.

Had it been Lisa?

Boyd?

She needed to get closer.

She walked to the end of the block and circled back once again, this time walking on the same side of the street as Lisa's house.

Then she had an idea. It was a stupid idea, and she knew it.

Bad, bad.

So, so bad.

A brisk wind blew crisp leaves around her as she approached the house. She scanned the street one last time. Looked for anyone watching out windows. But as before, she saw no one. Okay, so she was going to go for it. She was going to look into Lisa's window.

This is insane. You're *insane.*

Even as she heard the words in her head, she felt herself step from the hard sidewalk to the soft earth of Lisa's lawn.

Adrenaline flooded her body.

Just one peek. Just one. Just to see. Then I'm out of here.

Just one quick peek, then she'd drive back to Boston. After all, she was already here, and it had been a long drive.

Her boots sank a little deeper into the moist, cool earth as she got closer to the window.

This is a whole different league than Facebook stalking.

Seriously, you don't do stuff like this. Crazy *people do stuff like this. Peeping Toms and worse. This is such a violation of her privacy. His privacy. Their privacy.*

Their.

She hated that there was a word that meant both Boyd and Lisa.

This is so against the law.

Panic zigzagging through her, she whirled around, headed back toward the sidewalk, back to her car. But after a few short steps, she spun around again, her breathing short and shallow.

Christ, what the hell am I thinking? Doing?

Shaking with both terror and excitement, she finally reached the window. Stepping over a couple of mums, she flattened her back against the house.

If anyone saw her, she could quickly cut past the side of the garage and into the neighbor's yard. The streetlight cast wide shadows in that yard, and she could stay hidden most of the way back to her car.

Feeling a little safer with a plan, she focused on catching her breath. When she finally turned and stepped in front of the window, she found herself instantly staring directly into the living room.

Lisa was sitting on a brown-leather couch. She was wearing a black silk robe, and her blonde hair was piled loosely on top of her head. The light from the lamp next to her cast a warm glow over the side of her face, making her look almost angelic.

Chelsea's eyes took in the room. The decor was right out of a Pottery Barn catalog. The dark-leather couch and matching chairs formed a semicircle around a large wooden coffee table. Mud-colored pillows and matching throws accented the decor. The room was beautiful and well put together.

She watched the fire dance in the redbrick fireplace, its flickering light highlighting the expensive-looking, impressionistic artwork that hung on the walls. On the mantel were several framed photos.

Tears welled up in her eyes as she thought of the horrible contrast. This stunning, classy woman minding her own business and relaxing inside her upscale home. Looking like she completely belonged there in that magnificent house with her probably magnificent life. Then she,

Chelsea, wearing all black, her discount-store boots covered in mud, lurking in the shadows, trespassing on this woman's property. Shame flooded her, and she could barely breathe.

But she didn't leave. She couldn't pull her eyes from the scene before her. Not yet. She needed to see Boyd. She needed to see them together. How they acted together. Then she'd go.

She searched the room for any signs that Boyd might still live there, but she didn't see any. Just his car parked in the driveway.

Maybe that was a good sign. Maybe there was another reason for his car being in the driveway. Maybe he was dropping off the finalized divorce papers. Or it was a work-related visit.

Chelsea studied Lisa a little more. She had hoped Lisa wouldn't be as beautiful as her photos online. And that maybe, just maybe, there was something wrong with her. Some hideous deformity. But looking at Lisa now, through the glass, she could tell even from this distance that the woman was beautiful. Chelsea touched the ghastly scar on her cheek, more aware of it than ever.

When she saw Boyd saunter into the room wearing a T-shirt and sweats, she let out a small gasp. He walked toward Lisa, said something. Lisa frowned and said something back. Then he leaned down and planted a kiss on her cheek. Chelsea's world narrowed.

Oh, my God.

Her legs went rubbery.

Now she had proof. He *had* lied to her.

She'd been a fool to trust him.

Why had she been so damn gullible?

Her face burned. She was so done with him. She would drive back to Boston, and she wouldn't think about him ever again. He was a pig, an asshole. She never, *ever* should have—

Boyd's gaze swung to the window, and his eyes seemed to land on hers.

Chelsea ducked.

Oh, God.

Had he seen her?

She knelt next to the window frozen, unable to move.

Shit! Oh, my God!

Despite the cold, sweat popped out of her temples.

Oh, shit . . . please! You didn't *see me.*

She wanted to run, but her legs wouldn't move. Panic had its teeth in her.

She shouldn't have done this. She knew better. What was wrong with her? She squatted, talking to herself and waiting for what seemed like several minutes.

Okay, so maybe he couldn't see past the glass, she tried to tell herself. *With a light on inside, he would have just seen the reflection of the living room.*

She honestly had no idea if that was how it worked. If her logic made any sense. She waited for a couple of minutes, arguing with herself again, and when she didn't hear anything, she began to calm down a little.

Your imagination was just playing tricks on you, like it always does. He didn't see you. If he had, you would have known it by now.

Her frantic heartbeat slowing, she summoned the courage to stand. To look back in the window one more time. *Then* she'd head back to her car.

She stood. When she looked back through the window, Lisa was sitting exactly where she had been before, apparently undisturbed, but there was no sign of Boyd.

That was a good sign, right? After all, it had been a couple of minutes. If he'd seen her, he would have already come outside. Now she'd leave and never do anything this stupid again. She would stop stalking him . . . *them.*

Here.

Online.

Everywhere.

She'd delete his number from her phone. She would cut him out of her life completely, and—

A twig to her right snapped.

She froze, blood roaring in her ears.

She heard an angry whisper: "Chelsea?"

CHAPTER 19

THE NEXT EVENING Chelsea lay in bed, her chest aching. Her bedroom felt so cold.

She'd been lying in bed for several hours, but she had barely closed her eyes. Her mind was racing, and she couldn't think clearly.

How come happiness is so fleeting, yet sorrow is not? she wondered, wiping her tears away with the heel of her hand. Was that everyone's experience, or just hers?

Listening to the wet whisper of cars passing on the rain-slicked road below her apartment, she thought of the handgun. It was just mere inches away, tucked into the top drawer of her nightstand. Then she sat up, lit her bedside candle, and poured herself some wine, again nearing the bottom of a bottle. She took a sip and watched shadows dance across the wall.

Harry uncurled his lithe body and stretched. Then he walked over to her and nuzzled her neck, pressing his cold, moist nose against her face. He purred in her ear, trying to comfort her. She stroked him, then lay back down and turned on her side.

When Boyd had approached her in his yard the previous night, his eyes had glittered in the glow of a distant street lamp, and his tone had been sharp. He'd curled his fingers around her forearm and tugged her into the darkness.

"What are you doing?" he had whispered. His tone had been urgent, angry, and terrified.

She had been so taken by surprise, she'd just looked at the ground, her heart pounding in her chest, wishing for nothing else but to fall into a deep black hole and never, ever be seen again. To rewind time and rethink her stupid decision. To—

She'd looked him in the eye and seen the anger there. Maybe even a glimpse of disgust. "You told me you've been separated a year now. That your divorce was almost final."

"It was. I mean . . ." He shook his head. "Jesus Christ. Please. Just go. Now."

His words, the tone he'd used, the grip he'd had on her arm had sliced deep. She had bolted across his yard until her foot caught on something. She stumbled, fell chest down on the muddy grass. But he didn't come after her to help.

Maybe he hadn't seen her fall, had already gone back inside the house. And if he had seen, could she blame him?

No. Because no matter if he'd lied or hadn't lied, who did things like this?

Certainly not her.

Her mind hadn't been firing on all cylinders.

She blinked now in her room, her eyes finding the pile of muddy clothes on the floor. Falling in his yard had only added insult to injury, and she'd driven home, filthy, humiliated, and angry with herself for being so stupid. Why would he lie to her like that? And what else had he lied about?

A fly buzzed past her ear, probably attracted to some uneaten food on the nightstand. She swatted at it, unable to remember how long the food had been sitting there.

She looked up at the ceiling fan and listened to it roar with every revolution. Then she reached over to her nightstand and felt for the razor blade. She unwrapped it and pressed her finger against its sharp edge. She watched a bead of blood surface from beneath her skin. Although she couldn't fathom sticking her head in an oven like Sylvia Plath had done, she could certainly slice her wrists. She'd already done it once. And next time, she would get the job done right.

The horrible darkness was beginning to edge back into her brain, and she tried to push it away. She would not let herself sink into another debilitating depression. She would not allow herself to be swallowed up like that again.

She would get Boyd out of her head, once and for all. No texting. No stalking. No even thinking about him.

Her feelings for him had been too strong, and he'd lied to her, used her. So she was done with him.

She blew out the candle, and the room went dark and lonely.

Realizing her eyes were finally getting heavy, she carefully set the blade back on her nightstand and slipped into unconsciousness.

❂ ❂ ❂

Chelsea opened her eyes again when she heard her apartment door swing open. It was much later now. Moonlight streamed in through her bedroom window, bathing everything in the room in a bluish hue. Harry scrambled off the bed and scurried beneath it.

She glanced at the clock. It was almost midnight. She turned to her other side, her heart hammering in her chest. She'd been having another nightmare.

"Chelsea?"

A slice of light appeared beneath her bedroom door. Elizabeth had turned on the living-room light.

She heard Elizabeth muttering something to herself from the living room.

Chelsea squeezed her eyes closed.

There was a soft knock at her bedroom door.

"Chelsea?"

The door cracked open.

"Yeah," Chelsea said, her words sounding thick.

"Mind if I turn on the light?"

"Whatever."

Light flooded the room, and Chelsea squinted at the sudden brightness. She watched Elizabeth's gaze travel around the room, taking everything in. She was holding a Styrofoam container in her hand.

She sat on the end of the bed. "I just got back from the hospital. I brought some chicken and dumplings from the cafeteria. Have you eaten?"

Chelsea's stomach rumbled at the reminder.

She shook her head.

"Why don't you take a shower, and I'll heat some up?"

Chelsea crawled out of bed and shuffled to the bathroom on shaky legs.

As she ran hot bathwater and peeled her clothes off, she glanced at herself in the bathroom mirror. She hated what she saw staring back at her: a pale, haggard-looking woman with dark circles beneath her eyes.

She looked afraid.

And defeated.

Was she?

A minute later, she was in a hot bath with Epsom salts and a thick washcloth, scrubbing the awful night off her skin. As she soaked, she watched the steam rise from the water and tried not to think.

Twenty minutes later, her face washed, her teeth brushed, and wearing fresh cotton pajamas, she headed to the kitchen, passing the dirty dishes and half-full coffee cups that had been abandoned in various places around her apartment. She plopped down on a chair at the small bar and reluctantly told Elizabeth what she'd learned.

She cried as she talked and watched Elizabeth sip her coffee, the expression on her face morphing through a litany of emotions: concern, understanding, anger, concern again. But she didn't say one word. Finally, Chelsea stopped. She had confessed the whole awful story about last night. What she'd done. How Boyd had reacted.

After she finished, the kitchen was silent.

She looked at Elizabeth's pink scrubs. Tonight's had baby otters all over them.

After a long moment of silence, Elizabeth tilted her head and finally spoke. "Well, the good thing is that it's over."

Yeah. It was. There was absolutely no question about it.

"Sometimes you have to hit rock bottom to realize without a doubt that something was bad for you."

Yeah, I guess, Chelsea thought. A shiver ran through her.

Elizabeth went to the couch and grabbed an afghan. She draped it around Chelsea's shoulders. "Shake off the dust, and forget about that loser, okay?"

Chelsea nodded.

"It's over, and things are going to start looking up again. You are going to be just fine. *Better* than fine."

Chelsea wanted to believe it. But she had a feeling. A very strong one . . . that her friend was wrong.

CHAPTER 20

THE SUN WAS in its death throes as Lang sped along the quiet, winding road. He checked his handwritten directions to Katherine's house to make sure he was on the right route.

The address didn't show up on his phone's GPS, and the street signs—the few that he'd seen—were poorly marked. From the darkened storefronts, abandoned gas station, and boarded homes, it was clear the area had long been forgotten by most folks, which was a little surprising since the college was less than two miles away.

He made a quick call to Springfield, requesting updated information on Boyd Lawson. When he hung up, he downed more coffee. He was exhausted, and his back and knee were aching worse than ever. He cracked his window, letting cool air—and the pungent odor of wet manure—flood into the vehicle.

When he'd spoken to Katherine on the phone, she had seemed surprised to hear from him about the killings, but she'd agreed to meet. He'd been pleased she had, because his gut told him that meeting her would be important to the case.

He spotted the large horseshoe on a tree right next to a gravel path. It was where Katherine had told him to turn. His car bounced over the uneven path, fields of dense woods closing in on either side of his car. About twenty yards in, the path opened onto a large clearing where a gray, weather-beaten barn squatted. About a hundred feet from it was the charred remains of what appeared to be a farmhouse that had burned to the ground.

A double-wide trailer home sat a few yards from the barn. A gold Honda Accord was parked in front of it. Katherine had told him she'd be in her office in the barn, so he pulled to a stop beside it, next to a rusted-out tractor.

He parked and looked around, feeling a strange sense of déjà vu. The landscape surrounding him felt oddly familiar. He was trying to place it when the two white Dutch doors to the barn creaked open, and a woman that he presumed to be Katherine appeared.

The evening wind gusted, sending crisp leaves dancing at his feet as he stepped out of his car. Katherine pulled a blue jacket tight and smiled at him.

"You found me," she said.

"Thank God. If I got lost out here, I don't know if anyone would have ever found me."

She smiled and gestured for him to follow her back inside the barn. It smelled musty but with the sweet scent of old, decaying hay. A red door separated a room from the main area, and Katherine opened it, motioning for Lang to enter.

The office inside was clean, tidy, and surprisingly nice, considering its location. A large desk sat against one wall with a computer monitor and laptop situated on the wall opposite of it. A black-wood credenza held a large laser printer. A floor heater was buzzing next to the desk, but the place still felt cool and a little dank.

"This is quite a setup. You'd never know this was in here."

"Thanks. It was my mom's office."

Katherine was in her late thirties, a bit willowy, and had jet-black hair that was styled into a pixie cut. Before coming, Lang had learned she had spent eight years in the air force in an administrative position and now worked for herself.

Katherine opened a folding chair that had been leaning against the wall and offered it to Lang, then walked around her desk and sat in the high-backed leather swivel chair.

"Sorry," she said, pointing to his chair. "I don't typically get visitors."

"What is it you do again?"

"College textbooks. I compile and edit them."

"Interesting."

"Yeah, it can be. I probably have the equivalent of six or seven bachelor's degrees by now. For whatever that's worth. Which apparently isn't much." She smiled, but it didn't last long. "But that's not why you're here. You said there've been new developments in the Springfield case?"

Matter-of-fact and to the point. Lang liked that.

"That's correct. I'm trying to fill in any gaps from the last investigation."

"So, why questions about Chelsea Dutton?"

"Well, for one, I wanted to see if you could think of anyone who might have wanted to hurt her."

She frowned. "Like I told you over the phone, I didn't know her well. And I never heard from that other detective you mentioned—"

"Duplechaine."

"Right. I wasn't living here when my folks took Chelsea in." She wrung her hands, then dropped them on her lap. "I think I may have seen her only a few times."

"So that would be a no. You don't know of anyone who might have wanted to hurt her? A family member? Friend of the family? Friend? Anyone?"

"No, not that I know of."

"Can you tell me a little about her? The little bit that you saw?"

Her eyes flitted to the wall behind him for a moment. "She was shy, quiet. My mother told me she had had a tough life. Had been passed through a bunch of foster homes, and that's always hard on a kid. Mom worried a lot about her."

"How do you mean?"

"She seemed a little codependent. Followed my mother everywhere. Mom didn't think that was healthy."

"She was about eleven years old at the time, right?"

Katherine looked up, seeming to think about it. "Yeah, that sounds about right. Ten or eleven. To be honest, my parents didn't talk to me much about her or any of the other foster kids. I think they tried to focus mostly on me when I was around. Like they were worried I might think I was being ignored or replaced. They were very sensitive about things like that."

"Did you? Feel ignored? Replaced?"

Katherine gave him a slightly bashful look. "Well, at the time, I would've said no. But looking back, maybe a little."

"That's understandable."

Her eyes grew a little distant as though she was remembering something. "Yeah. I guess."

"And she lived here, what, six months?"

Katherine nodded. "Yes. Until the fire."

On the phone, Katherine had briefly told him about the house fire that had claimed both of her parents' lives. "I was sorry to hear about your parents."

Something dark passed in front of Katherine's eyes. She shrugged. "Thanks. But it was a long time ago."

"Still, I know it must have been tough on you."

"Yeah. I still miss them a lot."

"Did you see Chelsea at all after your parents died?"

"No." She cleared her throat. "Like I said, I barely knew her, so she never really entered my mind after that."

Lang asked her a few more questions, all of which turned out to be dead ends. Then they sat in silence for a moment.

"Anything else you think might help before I go?"

"Maybe. My mom kept very detailed records on all the foster kids. Any new prescriptions, problem behavior. That kind of thing. They were stored out here, so they survived the fire. I could get Chelsea's for you if you want."

"That would be great."

She stood and went to a file cabinet, opened one of the bottom drawers, and rooted around. A moment later, she was holding a pink manila folder.

The label read "Chelsea Dutton."

She handed it to Lang, and he opened it to find a bunch of loose pages and a spiral notebook.

"I remember when those murders happened," Katherine said, her arms crossed across her body. "I was stationed in Germany at the time and read about it on the Internet. It took me a while to realize she was the survivor everyone was talking about."

Lang nodded. He shut his notebook and stood to leave. "Thank you for your time, Ms. Jones."

"You're welcome. Sorry I wasn't more help."

Katherine walked Lang through the musty barn and back outside. As he limped to his car, he tried to process what he'd gotten from their conversation. At face value, it seemed to be nothing. So why had Duplechaine wanted to speak with her? Did he know something that Lang didn't? Or had talking with Katherine maybe been a lead that, in the end, Duplechaine decided wasn't worth the time and effort to follow?

His gut was still telling him the visit had been important. Maybe the file she'd given him would prove to be of help. While he'd been inside the barn, night had fallen, leaving just enough light for the tall oak trees to reflect off what appeared to be a pond far in the distance.

He lingered on the view again before stepping back into his car.

***

WHEN LANG PULLED up to his motel room, Janie was in the parking lot, leaning against her Toyota Prius, staring down at her phone.

Dammit, Victoria, he thought.

But when Janie looked up and smiled at him, he knew he couldn't be angry. At Victoria *or* Janie.

Victoria stuck her nose in his business because she cared. Moreover, he realized he was happy to see Janie.

He climbed out of his car and walked toward her, trying his best to mask his pain. He'd been driving way too much lately, which only served to intensify it.

"Well, isn't this a nice surprise." He smiled.

He took her in. She was such a beautiful woman in all the important ways. She was different from the women he'd dated when he was younger. Different from his late wife. But in many ways, better suited for him. Her looks were the icing on the cake. Her strawberry-blonde hair was casually pulled up in a high ponytail, and she was gripping her phone between her hands. "I won't interfere," she said, her eyes warm. "I'll stay out of your way. I'm only here to help."

Without saying a word, he pulled her into a hug and held her tight.

"I miss you," she murmured.

"I don't know why," he replied. He honestly didn't.

"Well, that's the thing. You don't need to."

He realized he'd missed her more than he'd thought.

She pulled away and looked him over.

"I can see you're in pain. Are you eating right? Resting?"

"Eh. You sound like Victoria. Why don't we talk about something else?"

He grabbed her bag and led her into his motel room. For most of the night, they held each other in bed. Janie filled him in on everything going on with her. She asked about the case and all the notes pinned to the wall. He explained everything that had happened since he'd been in Boston, and she had a bunch of questions. She was very familiar with the killings. Lang had been staying at her apartment the night they happened.

He'd always thought Janie would have made an excellent detective. Her deductive skills were top-notch. He was sure they rivaled some of the best in the business.

After they'd grown silent, he lay facing her. "I don't know why you put up with me."

She propped herself up on an elbow. "Are you kidding? You have excellent values. A great heart. You make me laugh. I like who I am when I'm with you," she said softly. "And on top of it all, you're very easy to look at."

"But I barely have a job. And I don't have much money."

"I can give a flip about money, Robert. You know that. Don't get me wrong. It's great to have the security of money. The freedom it affords me. But I'd give it all up to just have you."

He could feel a smile creep across his face.

"But don't make me chase you too long, okay?"

"Okay."

Neither of them was the mushy sort, so they left it at that.

Before falling asleep, he started reading through the folder Katherine had given him. Delores Jones had kept meticulous notes.

September 3

Nothing different. Chelsea still stays holed up in her bedroom unless forced to come out. She seems angry. And almost afraid we are going to hurt her. Pediatrician recommended medication. I'm checking with her caseworker as she has had bad results with similar medications in the past. She is very frightened at the prospect of just taking a vitamin. You would think that she thought we were trying to poison her. Poor girl. It just shows what she's been through.

September 5

This morning Chelsea turned a corner with us. She's never been receptive to touch. But this morning, she hugged me. I take this as a very good sign. I think we're winning her trust. We're going to keep doing what we've been doing. We haven't heard back regarding a decision on the medication yet. If it were my choice, at this point, I lean toward not medicating, at least until we see where this new behavior goes.

September 8

Chelsea has been following me around the last few days and helping with chores, like cooking and baking. She even helped muck out the barn yesterday. I've racked my brain trying to think if we've done anything different to promote this new behavior. We haven't. It's definitely trust. It just took her some time. Very excited about this.

Lang's phone rang. He looked at the screen. Sergeant Thatcher from the Springfield PD. He closed the notebook and took the call.

"Hey, got that information on Boyd Lawson you asked for," Thatcher said. The sergeant gave him a rundown on what he'd learned about his stints in rehab, then said he'd been pretty clean from a law-enforcement perspective over the last few years, aside from two speeding tickets. He worked for a car-detailing company called Fine Brush. Lived in Marblehead. Married to a Lisa Lawson—

Married?

Lang shook his head, wondering if Chelsea knew.

CHAPTER 21

WHAT THE HELL had she been thinking? Boyd wondered, his stomach twisted in knots.

Sneaking up to his house and spying in the window?

He splashed more Scotch into his glass, then slid the bottle back into the bottom drawer of his desk.

Why the hell would she do such a thing? She wasn't the stalker type. In fact, she was the most levelheaded chick he'd ever known. Yeah, he knew she'd had issues since the murders—and rightfully so—but shit.

What if Lisa had seen her?

How in the hell would he have explained it?

Like he didn't already have enough problems without Chelsea going completely batshit on him. The nonstop texting had been bad enough. Lisa still randomly checked his texts and voice mail messages. It was a deal they'd made in front of their couples' therapist six months ago. Honesty and trust, the therapist had said, were the foundation of all strong relationships, marriages especially. And Lisa had lapped up every bit of it.

While she didn't check his messages every day, he never knew when she would. And what if he hadn't had time to delete the damn things?

He sank back in his chair. Things had been going so great before that asshole Lang entered the picture. Before he'd shown up, reconnecting with Chelsea had been exactly what he'd needed. He'd wanted to do it for a very long time. He knew the first time he'd seen her that he wanted to know her better. Not only was she beautiful. There was just something about her. Something really special.

And he'd been right. She *was* special. Getting to know her better had confirmed it. She made him feel calm, appreciated. She was so damn easy to talk to. She didn't judge or pressure him. She accepted him for who he was, instead of holding her breath and waiting for him to become something he'd never been and never would be.

But then again, she didn't know the real him, did she?

His eyes slid over the room, taking in all the paperwork stacked on top of his desk. His white-laminate boards that contained strategy notes he'd taken more than six months ago. He hadn't applied even one of those brilliant new strategies since he'd written them down. They'd just sat there as words, great intentions, gathering dust. His Patriots dartboard was the most used item in the room.

He studied the elaborate crown molding, the ridiculous $1,000 window treatments that Lisa had insisted having installed in almost every room of their overly expensive house. Why had he let himself get so caught up in all this superficial stuff with her? All the designer trappings made him feel just that—trapped.

Everything about his life with Lisa was superficial. He hated it. If he were with Chelsea, he wouldn't have the same pressures to keep up with the Joneses. To have the latest and greatest upgrades. He wouldn't have to work his ass to the bone just to scrape by. Of course, Lisa made more money than he did. But he was still expected to pay the big bills and fund most of their lifestyle while she frittered away her Realtor income doing who knew what with her girlfriends.

For weeks, he'd been comforted by the fantasy of running off, living with Chelsea in her tiny apartment and her cheap IKEA furnishings. If he were with her, he wouldn't be under the pressure that was killing him now. And he'd definitely be happier.

But that couldn't happen.

It wasn't all Chelsea's fault. He knew that. Most of it was his own. He never should have lied to her. It was true that he didn't love Lisa—and even though he hadn't asked for a divorce yet, he *was* planning on leaving her.

One day.

Just not yet.

He hadn't meant to lie. The words had just tumbled out of his mouth at the farmers' market without any premeditation. Maybe it was a way of fantasizing about it. Of seeing how it felt to hear it spoken out loud. But from there, it took on a life of its own. He knew it hadn't been fair to Chelsea to lie to her about his marriage, and now he was wishing he'd thought through the repercussions before opening his big mouth. It was just another bad decision in a whole freaking lifetime of bad decisions.

Why the hell do I do things like this?

Some things he did made little sense. Surprised even him. And many of those same things ended up getting him into trouble. When he was a boy, he used to catch his father lying all the time. He'd watch him lie about big stuff, small stuff. To his mother, to colleagues he brought home to dinner, to the next-door neighbor. His father also lied to him. Boyd had hated it and promised himself he would never be like his father. But starting in middle school, he found that untruths just started rolling out of his mouth. He'd found it was sometimes easier, at least at first, to lie to impress people. To lie about his circumstances rather than actually change them. It was as though lying were in his blood.

But lying never came without a price. And the price had sometimes been steep.

Slumping back in his chair, he glared at the piles of contracts and schedules in front of him. He pushed away from his desk, letting his office chair roll into the center of the room.

He was behind on most of his appointments, all his sales goals, and he would have to answer to his father-in-law in less than forty-eight hours at their monthly staff meeting. He should never have been given a position with so much responsibility. He had been in over his head from day one.

Sometimes he suspected his father-in-law gave him so much responsibility because he wanted him to fail. It wasn't that he wasn't intelligent enough to do the job. It was just that his mind wasn't right. It hadn't been since the murders. Hell, that wasn't true. It hadn't been his entire life. He couldn't sit and focus on one thing for very long before anxiety overwhelmed him, and he needed a fix of some kind. And usually the fixes he chose just made it more difficult to focus.

He wished she'd told him about Lang. About him becoming involved in the investigation into the note. He would have extricated himself much earlier. The last thing he needed was to get involved again in that murder investigation. His jaw tightened when he thought about the way Detective Lang had stared at him at Chelsea's apartment. It was the same way he'd looked at him years ago. It was the same way his father-in-law still looked at him. And Lang threatened to stop by the house. If he did that, he would find out about Lisa. Then Lisa might find out about Chelsea.

He grabbed the liquor bottle again, splashed more into his cup, and wondered how he could untangle himself from the whole Chelsea situation. In the span of less than four weeks after she'd entered his life, he was already back on the police's radar. And that was the last place he needed to be.

It was all too much. And there was too much at stake. He could lose everything.

Just one more strike.

That was what Lisa had said when she'd caught him with some coke six months ago. And he knew she'd meant it.

Why do I do this shit to myself?

He ran his fingers through his hair and sighed. He didn't care so much about losing Lisa. That in and of itself would be a relief. But it was much more complicated than that. When Lisa's father found out, he'd fire him on the spot. And Lisa would surely take him for everything he had. The settlement wouldn't be about what was fair; it would be about what would hurt him the most. And in this town? With Lisa's family's influence? He would be hung out to dry.

"That better be the first one."

Lisa's voice startled him. She was standing in the doorway of his office, staring at him.

He spun his chair toward the door, inadvertently sloshing some of the liquor in his glass.

"Not only is it the one and only drink I've had; it's also heavily watered down." He pointed to a water bottle on his desk that hadn't been opened in weeks. He drank his liquor straight these days.

Lisa studied the glass in his hands, as though she was unsure whether to believe him. She was wearing a pink chenille sweater and black leggings with matching pumps—and her blonde hair was down, a silky curtain cascading across her shoulders.

He had always thought she was way out of his league. She was stunning, wealthy, ambitious, and smart as hell. But she was also cold and hard. He used to wonder if she ever regretted marrying him, but he didn't wonder anymore. He knew the answer. He saw it every day on her face.

"You agreed, Boyd. Never more than two drinks. And no more than twice a week."

He hated the clipped way she said his name. She always made it sound like something that disgusted her. It was probably her way of constantly reminding him that *he* disgusted her.

"You agreed," she said again, as though he also had trouble hearing.

Yeah, but I never specified the size of the drink.

"This is my first, and it will also be my last tonight. Scout's honor. I have an early morning."

Her eyes lingered on his, still judging, trying to figure out whether he was telling the truth. "I'm showing a house in a bit, then going out with Suzanne. Don't wait up."

"Great. Have fun."

She glared at him. "No more than two."

Boyd crossed his heart with his index finger.

She turned and left. As soon as Boyd heard the front door slam shut, he looked at his glass.

"If I'm just topping it off, it's always the first drink, right?"

He rolled his chair toward the desk, pulled out the bottle of Scotch again, and poured some more into his glass. He lifted it toward the front door in a toast. "To eternal first drinks, long may they last."

No one was going to emasculate him. He didn't care who she was. Or what she was holding over his head. But even as he thought it, he knew it wasn't true. She emasculated him all the time, and he was still there, living beneath the same roof. Taking handouts from her father. He wished he was stronger, braver. Not so much of an asshole. Or at least maybe not so self-aware.

He threw back the Scotch, enjoying the fiery slide of the alcohol as it traveled down his throat, and he finally started to relax.

But he knew it was temporary.

His thoughts circled back to Chelsea again. He was telling the truth when he told her he loved her. When he said he admired how strong she was and how much he'd thought about her over the years.

He remembered the first time he'd seen her. Ethan had stopped at the apartment to grab something, and she had been with him. He'd thought she was beautiful. Then he'd seen her again the night of the party.

Running into her at the farmers' market hadn't been an accident. He knew she went there every Saturday and had been watching her. And it hadn't been the first time. Over the years, she'd become another drug that he hadn't been able to kick. But now she was getting dangerous and could ruin it all.

Now he had to focus on making her go away.

CHAPTER 22

ELIZABETH SAT IN the car, staring out at the brightly lit home across the street from her. She'd driven to Marblehead to do something about Boyd once and for all. Since he'd reentered Chelsea's life, he'd done nothing but cause problems for her.

People like Chelsea were too sensitive to survive the real world alone. They needed people like her to intervene sometimes. To help them with the not-so-pleasant things in life.

She would never let Chelsea down like so many other people had in the past. And if things went as planned, Chelsea would never find out about this little visit. It would just be one of the many things Elizabeth didn't tell her. For her protection, of course.

As a child, Elizabeth had suffered a tremendous amount of pain and negligence. When she was barely two years old, her father had over-dosed on heroin, and she'd been left in the house with his body for two days. She remembered the flies, holding her ears to keep from hearing their loud, persistent buzzing, being forced to eat dog food and drink toilet water because she couldn't reach anything else. She remembered the foul odors of death and feces. Her mother had finally come home to find her toddling around in the house in only a filthy T-shirt.

After that, her mother had been negligent at best, usually two sheets to the wind on whatever she could get her hands on. When she was three, her mother had forgotten her in her car seat while she'd run inside the supermarket. It was ninety degrees Fahrenheit that day and at least twenty degrees hotter inside the car. She remembered calling out for her mother, over and over. Trying desperately to unstrap herself from the confines of her car seat while sweat gathered above her upper lip and formed between her shoulder blades and trickled down her spine.

She'd pounded on the side window every time someone would walk past, heading toward the store or leaving it. The scorching air had seared her lungs, making it difficult to breathe, making her very tired, and she had been just about to give up hope, about to let her eyes close, when a little boy with his mother finally had noticed her. She could still see the way he'd stared at her, his eyes wide with surprise. When the boy's mother had realized what was going on, she'd yelled to other people in the parking lot. Soon, a man had run over to the car with a jack. The sound of the heavy piece of metal smashing through the driver's side window had been deafening. Elizabeth had covered her face and clenched her eyes shut and only opened them again when she heard the passenger door opening.

That was the day she'd been ferried into the foster system. But, unfortunately, the system proved to be almost as awful as living with her mother. She'd seen her mother only once after that. She'd been six. Her mother had asked for visitation and shown up, hair greasy, mascara smeared, and smelling of stale cigarettes. She'd grinned, her teeth yellowed and crooked, and tried to give Elizabeth a cheap, glittery toy. Elizabeth had responded by spitting on her and turning her back. After that afternoon, her mother had never showed up again. Six months later, she found out that her mother had overdosed on pills and passed away.

But Elizabeth was tough. She could shoulder shitty things happening to her. She'd been built for it. Chelsea hadn't.

Elizabeth snapped back to the present. She glanced once more at the house and its high-class surroundings, then climbed out of the car and stuffed the keys in her coat pocket.

She rang the doorbell and immediately heard the sharp click of heels against a hardwood floor from inside.

Showtime.

A blonde woman whom she recognized as Boyd's wife, Lisa, opened the door wearing a charming smile.

"Hello. Tara, right?"

"Yes," Elizabeth lied, staring into the woman's blue eyes and accepting her slender hand.

A moment later, Elizabeth was inside a large sweeping foyer, listening to Lisa rattle on about the house she was selling. But Elizabeth wasn't interested in the house.

She was interested in Lisa.

She studied her, noting she had an upper-crust manner about her. She was also stunning. Elizabeth had found the house posted on Lisa's Facebook page, immediately called the number, and set up an appointment. Now, just a few hours later, she was here.

Lisa led Elizabeth deeper into the house. Even though she was wearing three-inch heels, her gait was fluid and graceful. Her perfume, smelling of honeysuckle, trailed behind her.

She reminded Elizabeth of those girls who used to taunt her. The ones who never cared how hard life already was for her. The girls who had been given everything since birth and had just flitted around without any real cares or worries.

"Live in Marblehead, Tara?" Lisa asked.

"Boston."

"Oh? So, you're looking to relocate?"

Elizabeth nodded, staring up at the chandelier in the high ceiling.

Lisa gave Elizabeth a tour of the downstairs, then led her upstairs. There were five bedrooms. The master bedroom was impressive. The king-size bed sat in a dark-wood canopy with light-blue bedding and what had to be dozens of ornamental pillows meticulously arranged on top of it.

"So, what's the asking price?" Elizabeth asked.

Lisa turned and looked at her pointedly, perhaps because she thought she should have done that bit of basic research already.

"Asking price is eight hundred seventy-five thousand dollars. No contingencies."

Elizabeth chuckled.

Lisa lifted her chin a little. She was reassessing her. Perhaps now questioning whether she was a viable client. When she spoke next, there was a hardness in her tone. "I assure you it's not only a competitive price; it's worth every penny."

Lisa finished showing the upstairs, then started for the stairwell. "Feel free to look around. I'll be downstairs finishing up some paperwork if you have any questions."

The guided tour was obviously over.

"My friend knows your husband."

Lisa froze on the top step. She turned around. "Oh?"

She gave Elizabeth a quick once-over again, and her eyes narrowed. "Your friend. Is he in the car-detail business?"

Elizabeth laughed again. "Well, he's a she. And no. I don't think it's a business relationship."

Elizabeth watched a vein throb in Lisa neck. It was clear she wasn't the type that got cheated on.

Lisa shot her a frosty look. "What's your friend's name?"

Elizabeth ignored her question.

"If I were you, I'd keep your husband on a short leash. I don't think you'd be happy about the kinds of things he does when you're not around."

Elizabeth bumped Lisa's shoulder as she pushed past her and started down the stairs.

"What's that supposed to mean?" Lisa called angrily.

Elizabeth turned. "Do you really need me to spell it out?"

Lisa narrowed her eyes but waited for her to go on.

"They're fucking each other."

Elizabeth climbed back in her car and started it up. As she pulled in to the road, she glanced at the house and saw Lisa peering out of the living-room window, frowning, her cell phone pressed to her ear.

She grinned, knowing she had just tossed a hand grenade right in the middle of Boyd's perfect little life.

CHAPTER 23

CHELSEA CAME AWAKE with a jerk. She peered around. Where was she?

The living room.

She was on the couch.

Wind gusted outside, and there were shadows on the walls. She looked at her watch: 9:00 p.m.

But why was she on the couch? She remembered retreating to her bedroom earlier that afternoon to lie down for a bit before sketching. Then she'd planned on making another dent in her transcription assignment. But she must have drifted off. Had she sleepwalked to the couch?

She pulled herself up into a sitting position, took a deep breath, and stretched as she looked around the room. It was still a disaster.

She shuffled slowly into the kitchen, picking up plates and trash along the way. She placed the dishes in the sink and righted the trash can. She could see that Harry had been digging around in it again. He'd cleaned the meat off two partially eaten chicken legs, and the bones now sat on her kitchen counter.

As she tossed the trash back inside the garbage can, she noticed several pieces of crumpled paper. She picked one up and smoothed it. It was one of her sketches.

Why would she have thrown one of her sketches away? She gathered the other crumpled-up balls of paper, went to the bar, and unfolded them all. As she suspected, they were all her sketches.

Why would she destroy her own sketches?

And why wouldn't she remember doing it?

Was she starting to black out again? A ripple of fear shot through her at the possibility. She hadn't blacked out for such a long time.

She smoothed out her sketches as much as she could and went to her closet, opened her safe, and slid them inside. Then she stood up and tried to figure out what she should do next. For a quick moment, she thought about checking Lisa's Facebook page to see if she'd written anything about the other night. Maybe she'd found out that Chelsea had been there and had written about her peeking through her window.

No, absolutely not. You are so done with her, him . . . them.

Feeling empowered by not giving in to temptation, she marched back to the kitchen and heated up more of her comfort foods: a Hungry-Man dinner with turkey and dressing and two turkey potpies. Elizabeth had said she should be kind to herself while she healed. That she should take it easy. So she was going to do just that.

While the food warmed, she took a long bubble bath and washed her hair with her favorite coconut-apple shampoo. She sat in front of the television and watched *Friends* reruns and binged on the enormous amount of food she'd fixed for herself.

Two hours later, her hair washed, dressed in clean pajamas, and so stuffed with comfort food she couldn't feel anything else, she crawled into bed and switched off the light.

CHAPTER 24

LANG CAUGHT HIMSELF smiling as he drove to Marblehead to talk again with Boyd Lawson.

He was thinking about Janie. He replayed the way she had kissed him last night. How great their conversation had been. It was always so easy to talk with her. He loved being around her, and her visit had reinvigorated him. He had hated to leave her this morning, but he had work to do.

Earlier that morning, he'd gotten ahold of a copy of Chelsea's visitor log from the psychiatric hospital and found out that Katherine hadn't been telling the truth during their meeting. Why would she have lied about visiting Chelsea? And if they hadn't been close, like Katherine had said, why visit her? He would need to make another trip to the farm to find out.

He thought about Chelsea and wondered again if she knew that Boyd was married. Delores Jones's journal had painted a picture of a frightened little girl who had endured unimaginable pain. So did Chelsea's DCF file. And then to have gone through the horrific ordeal of the attacks on her and her roommates. All of that was more than most people could handle. The last thing she needed was to be taken advantage of by a married man.

Just a mile or two out of Marblehead, Lang turned off Route 1A on to Route 129 and was immediately swept away by the beauty of Nahant Bay in the distance. Driving along the seawall, he lowered his windows and enjoyed the salty scent of the ocean. It was a sunny day, and the dark-blue waters stretched out to the horizon. Manicured parks and well-kept Victorian homes popped into view, lining the two-lane road. It was clear he had entered a more affluent area. The type of area he'd never be able to afford. But that was okay. He'd much rather live on farmland with a setup like Katherine's. He caught himself wondering if Janie would be happy with that. Maybe he should mention it. See what she thought.

He turned onto Ocean Avenue and checked his notes for the Lawsons' address. Once he reached the house, he pulled to the side of the street and peered into Boyd's circular driveway, noting the Audi SUV. He hadn't called before coming. He didn't like announcing himself. Never had. Surprise visits made people think on their feet, and he liked to see if they could keep their balance.

He knocked on the door, and a blonde he suspected was Lisa Lawson answered. She was wearing a pink bathrobe, and her eyes and the tip of her nose were red.

Lang introduced himself and showed her his badge. "Does Boyd Lawson still live here?" he asked.

She looked at him curiously. "Of course."

"Is he home?"

"No, but I expect him back any minute," she said. "Come in."

"That's kind of you, Miss . . . ?"

"Mrs. Lawson. Lisa Lawson."

Inside, he took in the home's extravagant high ceilings and dark-wood molding. The solid furniture. The place was as beautiful and elegant on the inside as it was on the outside. Lisa led him to the living room and motioned to the sectional. He took a seat, noting the buttery texture of the leather.

"Sorry about my appearance," she said. "I haven't been feeling so well today."

"I'm sorry to hear that."

She sneezed.

"Bless you."

"Thank you," she murmured, and turned her back to blow her nose. She faced him again. "May I ask what this is about?"

"Just tying up some loose ends on a case. I'm hoping your husband can help me."

"What kind of case?"

"A multiple homicide."

Lang told her he was from Springfield and was reinvestigating the coed killings. He offered the smallest amount of information possible, hoping Lisa would fill in the blanks with something he didn't know.

A grandfather clock behind her ticked loudly.

"Is he in trouble?" she asked finally.

Lang smiled. "Do you know something I don't know?"

She narrowed her eyes, obviously not finding any humor in his question. "No."

"I'm just following up on a conversation we had last week."

"Last week?"

"Yes, ma'am."

That piqued her curiosity. "So, you've spoken before?"

"Yes. In Boston. I take it he didn't mention it."

She stared pointedly at him. "We've both been so busy, we barely get a chance to catch up these days. I'm sure he meant to."

Lang nodded and decided to bait her a little more. "He said he had business in the city. That the car-detailing business was expanding."

Lisa blinked. Her eyes narrowed again. He could tell she was confused. She seemed to be waiting for more information, but Lang wanted to play his cards close to the vest. He looked around the living room.

"You have a beautiful home," he said.

"Thanks. When did you say you met him in Boston?"

"Last week."

She bristled. "Will you excuse me for a moment?"

"Of course."

Lang watched as she walked from the living room into the kitchen. With her back to him, she retied her bathrobe, pulling it tighter around her. Then she stood still as stone. Probably thinking.

Her robe looked expensive. Everything about Lisa looked expensive. She was an attractive woman, but he could see that she carried an air of entitlement about her.

"Would you like some tea or coffee?" she asked, not turning around.

"I'm fine, thank you."

"Water?"

"No, thank you."

A few moments later, she returned with a glass of water for herself. She sat on the recliner and offered him a tight smile.

"When you first got here, why did you ask me if he still lived at this address?"

"Just wanted to make sure."

They sat, silence growing between them again. He heard two birds fighting on the deck in back, then a car engine outside.

It sounded like Boyd was pulling in to the driveway.

CHAPTER 25

BOYD HAD MADE it a point to leave before dawn that morning while Lisa was still sleeping. He had left a note saying he had a sales call in Salem.

But it was just one more of his lies. He'd needed to get out of the house before she woke up. He knew she wanted to talk to him about something, and the thought of facing another of her suffocating interrogations was too much to stomach.

So he drove to Salem and ate a very early breakfast at one of his favorite diners. Afterward, he found a Home Depot and had a new house key made. His had mysteriously disappeared off his key ring. He had no clue how, but the last thing he needed was for Lisa to find out about it. She'd make a huge deal of it and find some way to blame it on his alcohol use. Before leaving the house, he'd slipped Lisa's copy off her key ring so he could get the copy made. She wasn't supposed to be going anywhere today, so hopefully she wouldn't notice it was gone before he could return it.

Over the course of the day, she'd called and texted at least six times, reiterating the fact that there was something important they needed to talk about, but she refused to tell him what it was until she saw him in person.

After he was done at Home Depot, he spent the rest of his day in the car, napping off and on. Sleeping was almost as good as the drugs and alcohol when he needed an escape. When he knew he couldn't put it off any longer, he drove back to Marblehead, rehearsing his story about his day. Whom he'd met. Where. What they'd talked about. He'd become an old pro at making up cover stories and had become way too good at it.

He had been on autopilot until he turned on his street, but was quickly jolted back to reality when he saw a strange Crown Victoria parked on the curb outside his house. His gut told him it was Detective Lang's car. After all, he had said he would be stopping by.

Shit!

Are you kidding me?

For a moment, he considered just passing the house, going somewhere else until the detective left. But the curtains in the front window were open. If they were in the living room, there was a good chance they'd seen him.

Christ!

He punched the steering wheel.

If it was Lang, what did he want? Why couldn't he have just called? Lisa was home.

What had he said to her?

He killed the engine and gathered his composure. Acting as casually as possible in case he was being watched, he climbed out of his car and walked up the sidewalk. As soon as he opened the front door, Lisa called to him from the living room.

He could tell by her tone that she wasn't happy.

He walked into the room, and there he was. Sitting on his damn couch. Lisa's glare cut right through him.

Christ. What have they been talking about?

"Hello, Boyd," Lang said, standing with a slight grunt.

Boyd was silent.

Lang extended his hand. "Sorry to drop in unexpectedly. I was just in the neighborhood and had a few more questions."

Just in the neighborhood, my ass.

Boyd reluctantly shook the man's hand.

"Nothing to worry about," Lang continued. "Just a few follow-up items. All very routine."

Boyd flicked his eyes sideways at Lisa again and saw she was still staring daggers at him. He looked back at Lang. "Let's go to my office."

Boyd led Lang into his study. He shut the door as Lisa watched from the hallway, her arms crossed tightly over her chest.

"You seem nervous," Lang said.

Boyd glowered at him. "You could have called."

Lang shook his head. "I hate phones. They're so impersonal." He looked at the couch. "Mind if I sit? My back is acting up something fierce today."

Boyd ran his fingers through his hair. "Sure. Whatever."

Lang took a seat on the couch and smiled up at him. "You've got quite a place here. Looks like you've done well for yourself."

"What do you need?" Boyd asked.

Lang pulled out his notebook. When he spoke, his voice seemed loud. "Your wife seems to be a lovely woman."

Boyd clenched his teeth.

"Does Chelsea know about her?"

Jesus. Could he have said Chelsea's name any louder?

Is Lisa still in the hallway?

Did she hear?

"Does she?" Lang asked again.

Adrenaline swooshed through Boyd's veins. "Yes," he replied through gritted teeth. *Now she does.*

Lang seemed to hesitate. "But I'm guessing Lisa doesn't know any-thing about Chelsea?"

Christ. "No."

"You told Chelsea you were in town looking to expand your business."

Boyd's face burned. "I was. *Am.*"

"Your wife seemed surprised by it."

Shit.

"I haven't told her."

"There is no expansion, is there?"

Boyd's stomach sank. There was no way he was going to get out of this. He shook his head and reached for his bottle of Scotch. "Want a drink?" he asked Lang.

"No, thanks."

Boyd poured his drink and decided to tell Lang the truth. About everything.

CHAPTER 26

BOYD STARED OUT the window, his mind spinning as he watched Lang leave. Everything was falling apart, and he knew he wouldn't be able to put all the pieces back together. But he was desperate to buy some time.

"Boyd!"

His muscles tensed. Lisa's voice was like nails on a chalkboard. Living with her this way was like dying a slow, painful death. He knew she had questions. Questions he didn't want to answer. He gulped down the last bit of his Scotch and hid the glass in a desk drawer.

He leaned over a document and pretended to be working as she flung open the door.

He swung his eyes to her. She stood in the doorway, still in her robe. Even though she was sick, she still managed to look great. He wished he didn't always notice these things about her. It would be so much easier if she wasn't so attractive.

She studied him, her glare slicing through his skin.

"You want to tell me what that was all about?"

"He was just following up on some information about those murders in college."

"What do you have to do with that?"

Boyd shrugged. "I was there, remember? I guess they have new information and are just double-checking things. Reinterviewing everyone. It's not a big deal."

"Why didn't you tell me you'd met with him before?"

He shrugged. "I didn't think it was a big deal."

"And why were you in the city?"

He didn't have an answer for that. At least, not one he could share with her.

"And what's this about the business expanding there?"

Sweat began to form on his upper lip. "I'm working up a proposal for your father."

She crossed her arms.

"You always talk about how you wished I took initiative. So that's what I've been doing."

"Let's see what Dad has to say about all of this," she said.

He knew she was testing him.

"He doesn't know. I've been doing it on my own. I was going to present it to him once I worked out all the details."

He met her eyes, wondering if she was buying it. If he could sell her for just a couple more days, he might be able to figure out a plan. A way to get out without getting totally gouged. Maybe liquidate a few things.

Her eyes were steady on his. "And why would the detective not think you were married?"

He tried to look baffled. "What?"

"I got the sense the detective was surprised we were married."

"Well, that's odd. But that's on him. Not me."

"But why would he think that?"

He lifted his hands in the air. "How am I supposed to know?"

Her frown deepened.

He was going to drown in his lies. He just knew it. His lies owned him now, and he wasn't sure how to disentangle himself. *If* he could disentangle himself.

"I met someone yesterday," Lisa said.

His mouth went dry. "Oh, really? Who?"

"A woman. She said you were in Boston last week fucking a friend of hers."

What the . . . ?

His skin flashed hot, then cold. "Who says things like that? That's crazy!"

"Is it?" she asked.

Lisa studied him, and he could tell she didn't buy his story. Hell, he wouldn't, either. But he couldn't cave. He knew how to lie as well as she knew how to read him. Still, it was taking all his self-discipline not to squirm in his seat.

"Who was it?"

"I'm not sure. She acted like she was interested in my listing on Chestnut. But she wasn't."

"Well, she's a liar. I can tell you that much."

"Is she?"

"Yes. She is. I'm not having an affair, babe. I would never do that to you. You know that."

Lisa's glare was unflinching.

"Who are you going to believe? Some lady you don't know or your husband?"

He regretted the question as soon as he asked it. He knew she'd never believed him. Not really. She'd also never believed *in* him. He was always guilty until proven innocent with her.

His head was pounding, and his thoughts were spinning. But he had to appear in control. He couldn't seem worried. If he messed this up, she could and would take everything. He hated how she had complete control. How he was completely dependent on her. Working for her father had been a terrible idea. He couldn't storm out. He couldn't tell her off. He was her bitch, and he hated her for it. He hated himself for it.

"Look, this is insane. All I do is work my ass off, Lisa. I work my ass off for us, and this is what I get?"

"There are too many—"

"Too many what?"

She raised her hands in front of her face. "Too many weird things happening at once. That detective. That woman telling me those things about you. And you're just trying to explain them away."

The room was silent, and Boyd wondered if she could hear his heart hammering in his chest.

"I'm going to get to the bottom of this, Boyd. Trust me. And you'd better be telling the truth."

She spun around and marched out of the room, slamming the door behind her.

CHAPTER 27

AT 11:00 P.M. Chelsea opened the door to find Boyd. He reeked of liquor, and from the way he was leaning against the side of the door frame, it was obvious he had consumed a lot of it.

She crossed her arms, anger flaring in her belly. Why was he here? To scold her again for peeping into his windows?

But she realized he didn't look angry. He was staring at the ground.

"You've been drinking."

He nodded. "Just enough to get the courage to come here."

"Why did you need to come here?"

Boyd looked up, making eye contact for the first time, but when he spoke next, his eyes flickered past her.

"For a lot of things, but mostly to apologize."

"For?"

"For lying to you."

She didn't say anything.

"I warned you I was an asshole," he said. "A couple of times."

That was true. He had. Numerous times. But she'd thought he was just being funny.

"I was telling you the truth about not loving her. I haven't for a very long time."

"But you're still married."

"Yeah."

"Were you ever even separated?"

"Yeah, I—" He stopped. He took a deep breath and shook his head. "No. Not yet, anyway. But I will be soon. It's just . . . it's complicated."

"It sounds simple to me."

"Well, it's not."

She didn't say anything.

"You deserve better," he said, his bloodshot eyes glistening.

"I know I do."

His eyes locked on the floor again.

"Why are you here, Boyd?"

He stuffed his hands in his pockets and shifted his gaze to her doorjamb. "I just . . . I needed to see you."

"Well, you've seen me now, so . . ."

"I want to be with you. To talk to you."

He seemed so vulnerable. It reminded her of the Boyd she'd thought she had known. But that Boyd had never existed. He'd been a lie.

He stared at her. "I know what I did was wrong. Lying to you like I did. And I'm so very sorry. But I wasn't lying about everything. I wasn't lying when I said I care about you. That I love you. I know it has to sound strange, since we haven't known each other very long, at least intimately, but I never stop thinking about you, Chelsea. Never."

She wanted to believe him. But he'd lied. A big lie. And she had no clue what else he'd lied about. Or would lie about in the future. She wasn't willing to go through the pain of finding out.

"You lied to me. I can't trust you. I'd never be able to trust you."

He shook his head. "Chels, that's not—"

"We're done," she said.

She grabbed the door, and he stepped back into the hallway.

"Chelsea, please. Give me another chance."

"For both of our sakes, don't come back," she said. "I mean it." She swung the door shut and engaged the locks.

CHAPTER 28

IT WAS HALLOWEEN, and Chelsea was on edge. She drove a nail into the wall with a small utility hammer, then carefully hung the second of her framed sketches. Stepping down from the couch, she looked to see if it was level.

She'd meant to frame and hang her sketches months ago and was glad she was finally getting around to it. There was something soothing about the rural landscapes she'd drawn. And she desperately needed soothing today. She was hyperaware that it was Halloween, and the fifth anniversary of the murders.

She studied her drawings and thought about how proud she was for standing up to Boyd. It had been liberating. And it had provided closure. There was still lingering pain, a lot of it, but it would probably just take time.

Someone knocked on the door.

She frowned. Surely Boyd wasn't coming back again after what she'd told him. She set a third framed sketch on the couch, then went to the door and peeked through the peephole.

It was Detective Lang.

She unlocked the door and opened it wide.

"Good morning," Lang said. "I hope I'm not disturbing you."

"No. Not at all. Come in."

"I just had a couple of quick questions, if you don't mind."

"I never mind."

She motioned to the small kitchen table, and he had a seat.

"Coffee?"

"Sure."

She opened a cupboard and grabbed two mugs.

"Does the name Katherine Jones ring a bell?" Lang asked.

Her stomach suddenly clenched, but she wasn't sure why. "I . . . I don't think so."

"I received a copy of your visitor log from the time you spent in the psychiatric hospital and saw that she visited you."

Chelsea handed Lang his cup of coffee and sat down.

"I don't remember that. Are you sure?"

"Positive. It's in the log."

She shrugged. "Honestly, I have no idea who that is."

Lang eyed her and looked as though he was going to say something else but then decided not to. He looked down at his notebook, and she saw that there was something he'd drawn several circles around.

"I was also rereading Boston PD's reports, and there is a name that I'm not familiar with. Elizabeth Jessup. Who is she?"

"Yes, Elizabeth. She's my friend."

"And she was here when you found the first note?"

She wondered why he was asking. "Not when I found it but afterward. She lives here in the building. Why?"

"Just filling in some holes. The more information I have, the better. How long have you known Elizabeth?"

"Close to five years now. We met at the psychiatric hospital in Springfield."

"She was a fellow patient?"

164

Chelsea shook her head. "Elizabeth? God, no. She was a nurse. She still is, here in the city."

"So, you both moved to Boston from Springfield?"

"Yes."

"How did that work out?"

"Elizabeth was offered a job out here, and a couple of weeks later, I followed her. I really wanted to get out of Springfield, away from everything that happened, and knowing I'd have a friend in Boston already, a close one, it seemed like it would be the perfect place to go."

"What unit does she live in?"

"Six D. It's just up the stairs."

Lang scribbled the information down.

"You have a phone number for her?"

"Yeah." She gave it to him, and he wrote it down.

Harry pressed against her leg and mewed loudly. "Are there any new developments on Ethan?" she asked, bending to pick up the cat.

Lang didn't answer her.

When she straightened, she noticed Lang was staring at the sketches she'd hung. He stood up and moved closer to them.

"You said you drew those, right?"

"Yeah."

He picked up the sketch on the couch and studied it for a long moment. She wondered why he was so interested in it. Although she loved it, it wasn't particularly well drawn—it was just a drawing of old farmland.

"I've got to get going," he said suddenly. He set the sketch back on the couch and limped quickly to the front door. "Thanks for your help. I'll call you soon."

CHAPTER 29

LANG LEFT CHELSEA'S apartment and sped the two hours back to Katherine's farm in Springfield. He'd already had plans to go there today to ask her about the visitor log, but he had wanted to check in with Elizabeth Jessup first. Then Chelsea's sketches had changed his mind.

Right now, he had a hunch. And hunches in his experience were usually gold. He'd always had a great sense of intuition, something that his father, who had also been a detective, had also had. Both his father and another late mentor of his had long ago told a very green Robert Lang that intuition was the secret ingredient that separated the best in the field from everyone else.

And if his hunch was wrong?

At the very least, he would find out why Katherine had lied about visiting Chelsea at the hospital.

He considered calling her, to make sure she'd be home when he got there, but decided against it, once again wanting to capitalize on the element of surprise.

As he drove west on Interstate 90, he replayed his previous conversation with Katherine in his mind. When he had asked her if she'd seen Chelsea since the killings, she was very clear about the fact that she had not. Yet her name had been on the visitor log. According to the records, she had visited Chelsea one week after the killings and had stayed for fourteen minutes.

Again, why would Katherine lie about seeing Chelsea?

If they hadn't been close, why had Katherine visited her? And why such a short visit?

There was something she wasn't telling him, and he needed to find out what. And then there were Chelsea's sketches. Chelsea seemed to have pulled her memory of the farm from her subconscious and drawn it. Numerous times. Lang wondered if that was a sign of something.

Reaching the farm, he bounced along the dirt path. When he got to the clearing, he felt a stab of disappointment.

Katherine's car was gone.

He had gambled on surprising her, but this time he'd lost.

He parked next to her trailer, climbed out of his vehicle, and stretched his legs. Massaging his lower back, he called her cell phone, but it went straight to voice mail.

Damn.

He left her a message and then decided to look around outside.

He surveyed the perimeter of the trailer home. Other than a small grill that looked like it had seen better days, a folding chair, and a lot of crisp, brown Kentucky bluegrass, there wasn't much to look at. He walked around the barn and found a rusted-out tiller and a few other pieces of long-abandoned farm equipment nestled in overgrown brush. Nothing of interest.

He walked to the pond, his mind turning everything over again. The pond was much larger than he'd originally thought. It was oval and framed on three sides by large trees and high weeds. The waterline today was extremely low, due to the lack of rain in Springfield over the summer and fall. It was the biggest drought Springfield had experienced in more than a decade, and six to eight feet of dark mud separated the thick reeds from the water's edge.

Lang started to walk out onto the fifteen-foot-long dock but noticed many of the boards looked rotten. So instead, he walked around to a little clearing that gave him easier access to the bank.

He and his father used to fish together a lot when he was a boy in Alabama. They'd often take turns seeing who could skip a rock the farthest on Lake Guntersville. Whoever got his rock all the way to the other bank won. His father won most of the time back then, but today Lang would be unchallenged. He searched the bank for the perfect flat rock and bent to pick it up. Ignoring his back's protests, he skipped it across the pond's glistening surface and watched the ripples disrupt the flawless reflection of the surrounding trees.

Smiling, he reached into his pocket for his cell phone and tried Katherine again, and once again was sent to voice mail. The afternoon was mild for this time of year and the sun was strong, so he decided to sit beneath a large oak and make a couple of calls. The first to Elizabeth Jessup. When he dialed the number, he received a message that the number was out of service.

Odd.

He tried it again.

And got the same message.

Maybe he'd written the number down wrong. Or maybe Chelsea got the numbers confused. These days everyone's numbers were in speed dial. They didn't have to memorize much.

Watching a bird skim the pond's surface in search of a meal, he tried someone else. Dr. Swenson, a psychiatrist who had been listed in the file that Delores Jones had kept about Chelsea. Dr. Swenson's notes hadn't been included in the paperwork that the Department of Children and Families had given him. Unfortunately, mistakes like that happened often with case files. People were responsible for the information they contained. People were human. They made errors.

Per Delores's notes, Chelsea had seen Dr. Swenson a total of six times. He left the doctor a voice mail, explaining why he was calling.

Talking with Dr. Swenson was certainly a reach, but since Chelsea's memory of those days had been partially erased, he hoped the doctor could shed some light on her past. People who might have treated her badly while in foster care. Maybe she'd even mentioned Katherine to him. If Dr. Swenson agreed to meet, Lang was certain Chelsea would consent to the meeting. Then he called Garcia and asked for some basic background on Elizabeth Jessup.

The wind picked up, and he started to get cold. He decided to go back to his car and wait. He'd either wait for Katherine to return home or find out where she was so he could meet her.

As he was in the process of standing, he spied another great rock, flat, a little smaller than the palm of his hand. He stopped and picked it up. The weight was perfect. About the weight of a tennis ball. He windmilled his arm to limber it up. He knew he'd probably regret it, but for old times' sake, he took a deep breath, got a running start, and flung the rock with a side pitch as hard as he possibly could.

Just as he'd thought, his back screamed. But he was getting used to that. The afternoon sun reflected brightly across the water and made it difficult to see very far, but he kept his eyes peeled on the waterline.

He saw the first splash. Then another ten yards farther. Then another. The rock bounced past a thicket of weeds in the center of the pond, then:

Ching!

Lang was surprised by the sound. The rock had hit something. And from the sound of it, something metal. He squinted out over the lake and saw the ripples on the far shore, close to the frayed remains of an abandoned rope swing. Then a glint of silver flashed in the sunlight.

He limped around the pond quickly, keeping his eye trained on the area where he'd heard the sound as he navigated the tall, thick reeds and cattails along the edge of the pond. When he finally got to the other side, he looked at the water about twenty feet out and saw what the rock had hit.

"Son of a bitch."

Lang yanked his phone out of his pocket and made a call.

CHAPTER 30

AROUND 11:00 A.M., it began to storm, and Chelsea found herself having darker thoughts than she'd had for weeks. Maybe months. She sat on the couch, wrapped in her afghan, and sipped wine.

Elizabeth turned toward her from the recliner, concern creasing her face. "You okay?" she asked.

No. "Yeah," Chelsea said.

Elizabeth was well aware of how Halloween affected her, so she'd gotten there early and was doing her best to distract her. She'd brought three documentaries to watch and a big spread of food. Chips, hummus, sour cream and onion dip, a plate of nachos. She'd also filled the freezer with potpies and TV dinners. All Chelsea's favorites.

Chelsea had already eaten a ton of food. After all, who the hell cared if she got fat? It was more important to feed the pain right now. Crowd it out so nothing else could fit.

Network television was airing a special of the fifth anniversary of the Springfield Coed Killings tonight, so they were having a documentary marathon instead. They were now on their first DVD: *Inside Job*, a documentary about the financial crisis of the late 2000s. But Chelsea couldn't get into it. She wouldn't be able to get into any of the DVDs today. She was glad Elizabeth was there, though. That she wasn't alone.

Since Lang had mentioned the name *Katherine Jones*, Chelsea hadn't been able to stop thinking about it. She experienced a visceral reaction almost every time the name flashed into her head. Twice today she'd vividly smelled the odors of gasoline and fetid pond water. But why?

Elizabeth paused the DVD and turned toward her. "If you ever had to go away, somewhere . . . anywhere, where would you go?"

The question seemed totally random. It had come out of nowhere. "Why would I have to go away?" Chelsea asked.

"It's hypothetical."

"I don't know. Why? Where would *you* go?"

"I'm thinking Florida. Like down in the Keys somewhere. I've been checking it out online. It's beautiful down there."

Is this Elizabeth's idea of a distraction? she wondered. Or was she thinking about going away?

Her mouth went dry at the possibility that her friend might be thinking of leaving.

Was Elizabeth getting bored with Boston?

Bored with *her*?

Every time they got together, they did the same things. Maybe that was why she'd picked up extra nursing shifts lately. Because she was bored. Elizabeth was definitely more adventurous than Chelsea was. She often went out to dinner with nurses she worked with, as well as other colleagues. But she still seemed to always be there when Chelsea needed her. Was she getting weary of Chelsea's dependence on her? Or were her concerns right now just wine fueled?

"Are you getting tired of being my friend?" Chelsea asked, searching.

"Huh?" Elizabeth asked, a chip in her hand. "Why would I get tired of being your friend?"

"Because we just do this." Chelsea motioned to everything around them. "Sit around my apartment, staring at a screen and gorging on crappy food all the time."

"But I love doing this," Elizabeth said. "Of course I don't get bored with it."

"We can go out to dinner sometime. Do something different, you know?"

"Sure. But I don't really care either way."

"So, that's not why you're talking about going away somewhere?"

"No. Like I said, it was just hypothetical."

"Are you sure? It's not because you're getting bored hanging out here?"

"Mm-hmm. Positive." She stuck the chip in her mouth.

Her cheek didn't jump. She was telling the truth.

Chelsea took another sip of wine and stared out the French doors. "Detective Lang stopped by earlier. He said he wants to talk to you."

Elizabeth straightened in her chair. A strange look crossed her face. "Why?"

"Because your name was on one of the police reports. I guess he wants to talk to anyone who was around at the time."

Elizabeth didn't say anything.

"Also, when Lang was here this morning, he asked me if I knew someone named Katherine Jones. The name didn't ring a bell. But it's weird, because when he said the name, I got this really funny feeling. And now I can't get the name out of my head."

CHAPTER 31

ELIZABETH DUCKED DOWN in the front seat of her car as Boyd's headlights flashed as he drove past her. She'd just watched from three blocks away as he'd burst from his house and jumped into his car. He had been in a big hurry.

She'd left Chelsea sleeping at her apartment. Chelsea drank the entire bottle of wine all by herself before 2:00 p.m., then had vomited it all up—along with the enormous amount of food she'd eaten. She'd put Chelsea to bed with some Valium, then driven out to Marblehead. It was barely 4:00 p.m. now, but the sky was prematurely dark due to an approaching storm.

As Boyd's car disappeared around a corner, she felt the fury rise inside her again. She was pissed at herself. She should never have let things go so far with Boyd. No, she never should have let it happen in the first place. She wasn't happy that it had to come to this, but Boyd had left her no choice.

He wouldn't leave Chelsea alone and was going to ruin everything. She had hoped her first visit with Lisa would have done the trick and kept him away. But it hadn't. So now she was being forced to take more drastic measures. Boyd was once and for all going to stop screwing with Chelsea's head.

Elizabeth drove the car to a neighboring street and parked. Then she stepped out of the car. A bitter wind roared through the trees and stung her eyes as she walked up the street toward Boyd's house as inconspicuously as possible. She plunged her hands inside her sweatshirt pockets. She clutched a key to Boyd's house in one hand. A knife was in her back jeans pocket.

She'd taken Boyd's house key the last time he had stayed over at Chelsea's apartment. He and Chelsea had been sleeping in her bed when she'd stopped by. When she'd removed it from his key ring, she wasn't yet sure what her plan would be, but as usual, her instincts had proven right. The key was about to come in very, very handy.

She looked around one final time, then walked up the sidewalk that led to his porch. The house was dark except for a light glowing from a second-floor window that she guessed was the master bedroom. She knew for a fact that Lisa was home because she'd watched her pull a pair of curtains closed half an hour ago.

She slid the key into the lock and turned it gently until she heard a soft click. Then she pushed on the door, wincing as the hinges squealed. After opening the door a little wider, just enough to slide in, she quietly shut it behind her, then turned around and gave her eyes time to adjust to the dark.

The entryway was massive, but she wasn't able to see much else. Just the soft light from upstairs, at the top of a wide staircase.

Blood pounded in her temples as she crept slowly, carefully up the stairs. When she reached the top landing, she surveyed her surroundings. In the dark, she could make out a long hallway with four doors. Most of the doors were at least partially open. A light was on in one of the rooms. The master bedroom.

She moved carefully toward the door. When she reached it, she leaned up against the wall and peeked through the crack. Lisa was lying across her bed, reading a magazine. Her hair was pulled up in a loose bun, and she was dressed down in a T-shirt and yoga pants.

Elizabeth pulled the knife out of her back pocket and took a step sideways. A floorboard creaked beneath her foot.

She froze.

She heard movement from inside the room.

"Boyd? Is that you?" Lisa called.

Elizabeth took a deep breath, then exhaled even deeper.

"Boyd?" Lisa called again.

The room went silent.

Elizabeth heard the box spring squeak as Lisa climbed off the bed, then soft footsteps as Lisa padded toward her.

Sweat beaded at Elizabeth's hairline. She tightened her grip on the knife. It was showtime.

CHAPTER 32

"WHAT THE HELL is going on?" Boyd mumbled to himself, his pulse drumming in his throat. He looked down at his phone, waiting impatiently for another text message to come through. As soon as he'd received the text message, he'd jumped in his car. Now he was sitting at a bar called Leo's, a dive in East Boston.

"Another one?" the bartender asked. She was old and had a thick Irish brogue. He looked up at her, not comprehending what she was saying. Too many thoughts were bouncing around inside his head, swirling and kicking up dust like a tornado. He stared, unseeing, at her coarse red hair. It was threaded with gray strands and was sculpted into one of those beehive hairstyles popular decades ago. A big blue pin in the shape of a butterfly poked out of it.

"What the hell is going on?" he asked himself again.

"Another whiskey?" she repeated, more loudly.

"Oh. Yeah, sure."

She topped off his glass.

Leo's was dark and mostly empty. Other than the Tom Jones song playing quietly on the jukebox a few feet away, the place was quiet.

Serious drinkers only.

Boyd's hand shook as he raised the glass to his mouth.

He had been busy, arguing with Lisa, as usual, when the text came in. He hadn't recognized the number, so he'd ignored it at first. But when Lisa started in on him about how she didn't believe a word he said and knew that he'd been cheating on her and that he needed to get his shit out of the house immediately, *then* went on a long, tiring diatribe about how worthless he was, the phone served as an excellent distraction.

He certainly never expected the text to say what it did. Seeing the name on the screen jarred him and transported him right back into the past.

> We need to talk. Drive to Boston and find a bar. Once you're there, text me your location. If you tell anyone about this, get the police involved, or do anything else stupid, Chelsea's blood will be on your hands. I mean it. —E

Lisa had still been ranting as he'd jumped up, grabbed his wallet and keys, and left the house.

It had been two and a half hours since the text had come in. He'd texted Ethan back twice, telling him he was at Leo's. But he hadn't gotten a response yet.

Where had Ethan been hiding all these years? Was Chelsea in danger? Was *he* in danger? What did Ethan want from him? Where was he?

Boyd had started to call the police twice, but both times he'd stopped one digit short, remembering Ethan's words: *Chelsea's blood will be on your hands.*

What the hell?

Was Ethan watching him now?

Boyd scanned the bar. There were only two other patrons. An old man staring deeply into his nearly empty glass, looking as though he'd rather be six feet under than where he was, and a woman in an oversize fur coat who was quietly nursing a beer.

Boyd promised himself that if he got out of this in one piece, he'd go home, pack a suitcase, and just leave. He'd let Lisa have everything and just start fresh. He didn't care if he had to bartend for a while, wait tables. He'd do whatever it took. He'd move somewhere else. Change his ways. Become honest for once. He'd learned his lesson the hard way.

He stared down at his phone.

Why hadn't Ethan texted back yet?

He sat impatiently nursing his drink, waiting for another text.

CHAPTER 33

TWO TWENTY-FIVE-FOOT-TALL SPOTLIGHTS illuminated the pond like a football field as a police diver signaled to the tow-truck driver. The truck clanked and grinded as its pulley slowly turned.

Lang stood on the water's edge along with about a dozen police officers, mechanics, and four men in hazmat suits. They all watched as the vehicle was slowly dragged out of the pond.

Lang's heart pounded as he recognized the car as a silver Lexus. The same make, model, and color as Ethan's car.

Holy shit.

As the car neared the shoreline, Lang could make out something, or someone, in the passenger seat. He stood back as the men in the hazmat suits went to the vehicle. It would be a while until there was a positive ID, but Lang already knew who was in the car.

Ethan.

After all this time, they'd finally found him.

Did Katherine know about this? Was this why she'd lied about visiting Chelsea after the killings?

Lang waited patiently as the forensics unit gathered evidence and carefully removed the decomposed body. He studied the remains. The body was slimy and almost completely void of flesh. Green-brown algae had grown over much of it. Other than the basic shape, there was nothing human left of it at all.

One of the men in a hazmat suit approached Lang.

"Victim is unidentifiable. No wallet or identification. Papers in the glove box are all but destroyed. We're going to do a full sweep of the rest of the pond to see if we can find anything else."

Lang nodded, then tried Katherine's number again. Again, he was put through to voice mail.

An hour later, the remains were being transported to the chief medical examiner's office. Detective Miller from the Springfield PD walked up to Lang. "Katherine Jones was picked up in Boston about thirty minutes ago."

"Boston? Where?" Lang asked.

"Office building downtown. Her vehicle was spotted in a parking lot. They have her en route to District D-4 for questioning. Warrant also came in to search the property."

"Thanks."

Lang watched as the supervising officer barked orders to start searching the premises.

He rubbed his chin. Katherine was in custody in Boston, so that was where he needed to be.

CHAPTER 34

LANG LIMPED INTO the Boston station, his back and knee on fire with every step. The station was musty and old, with fluorescent lights that cast a blue-gray pallor over everything. Uniformed police officers walked in and out of the bustling station, some of them escorting gang members, prostitutes, and drunks—two of them loudly proclaiming their innocence.

Lang pushed past them all until he reached the reception desk. The officer sitting behind it looked at Lang with a detached, world-weary gaze.

"Can I help you?"

Lang flashed his badge and explained who he was, then asked where Katherine Jones was being held. The officer gazed curiously at Lang and picked up a phone. He spoke in hushed tones, and almost as soon as he hung up, Detective Garcia emerged from one of the doors at the far end of the room.

"Lang," he called. "Damn, how did you make it here so fast?"

"Getting used to the drive."

"Damn, man."

Lang ignored him. "Let's go talk to Jones."

"Can't. She's lawyered up."

Shit.

He had hoped to speak to her before she sought counsel. Now everything would be filtered and measured.

"It doesn't matter, anyway," Garcia said. "Her alibi is airtight."

"No alibi is airtight," he said. But it was just a reflex. He knew she wasn't a suspect. But he also knew she'd been withholding information.

"Her alibi is," Garcia continued. "She was in Germany at the time of the homicides. Air force. It all checked out."

Lang remembered. But he still wanted to speak with her.

"Did anyone else have access to the property when she was stationed in Germany? A relative? Friend?" he asked Garcia.

Garcia shook his head. "We didn't get that far. But look, her lawyer just wants a half hour with her. And that expires in"—he glanced at his watch—"about fifteen minutes."

Lang processed Garcia's words, realizing that would give him enough time to try calling Chelsea's doctor again. He also needed to call Chelsea to double-check Elizabeth Jessup's phone number. The one she'd given him was obviously wrong. "Okay. I'm going to step outside to make a quick call. I'll meet you back here." Pulling his phone from his pocket, Lang started for the heavy double doors that led out of the station.

"Lang!" Garcia called. He snapped his fingers. "You also asked about Elizabeth Jessup."

Lang spun around a little too fast, sending a bolt of pain shooting up his back. He clenched his jaw.

"You sure you got the name right?" Garcia asked. "I couldn't find anything on her. I even checked with Springfield Medical, and human resources says there's no record of anyone ever working there by that name."

A chill crept up Lang's spine.

Something wasn't right.

"Want me to run a full background check?" Garcia asked.

"Yes, please," he said, adrenaline flooding his veins. He turned, heading back toward the station's entrance. "I'll be back. I need to run real quick and check something out."

"How long?" Garcia asked.

"Thirty minutes. An hour, maybe."

"It can't wait?"

"No."

"I don't know how long I'll be able to hold Miss Jones."

Lang limped toward the door. "I'll be back as soon as I can."

CHAPTER 35

Meet me at Chelsea's apartment in thirty minutes. Don't
be late, and don't be stupid. If you tell anyone or bring
anyone, it's going to get messy.

Boyd read the text several times, goose bumps breaking out on his
arms. His heart was racing so fast, he could hardly breathe.

What the hell was going on?

What did Ethan want from him?

And why him?

"Want another?" the bartender asked.

"No." He pulled a twenty from his wallet and threw it on the bar.
He took a deep breath, downed the rest of his drink, and headed out
the door.

CHAPTER 36

ELIZABETH WAITED IMPATIENTLY in Chelsea's kitchen, trying to stifle a yawn. She'd just checked on Chelsea in her bedroom. She was in a deep sleep, courtesy of the special cocktail of pills she'd given her. Now, with most of the lights off, she stood by the kitchen counter and waited.

What she was about to do would be risky and had to be handled delicately. She'd taken the necessary precautions in case things didn't go as planned. She'd found a secure place and had stashed a change of clothes, a fake ID, and other important papers with the money she'd collected from Chelsea's fireproof safe. It would be enough to keep them going for more than a few months if that was what it came down to.

But she hoped it wouldn't.

She didn't like that she had to do this. It was dangerous, especially with Lang breathing down everyone's necks. In the past, she'd gotten lucky, but she also knew that luck had a tendency to run out.

Shit!

Her job would be so much easier if Chelsea would have just listened to her and hadn't gotten back in touch with fucking Boyd. She'd had a feeling this would happen.

All these years, she'd worked hard to keep Chelsea from spiraling, from feeling most of the pain she otherwise would have had to feel.

But now Chelsea was making it so difficult.

A knock on the apartment door jolted her from her thoughts. "Come in," she called, and curled her fingers around the gun's grip. Adrenaline surged through her veins as she watched the doorknob turn.

The door swung open, and Boyd appeared in the doorway.

"Hello? Why's it so dark—"

"Close the door," she commanded.

He peered in her direction and turned on the light.

Seeing the gun, he froze and lifted his hands in front of him. Even from a distance, she could smell liquor on his breath.

What a loser. Even drinking at a time like this.

"What the hell?" he asked, clearly startled. "What are you—"

"The door," she snapped, her pulse throbbing in her ears. "I said to close it!"

He did as she asked. His eyes scanned the living room, over her shoulder, deeper into the kitchen behind her.

"Why do you have a gun? Where's Ethan?"

"Sorry. He had other plans."

He stared at her. "I'm confused."

"No shocker there."

Boyd looked even more confused. "But I—"

"Come on. There must be a brain somewhere in that pretty head of yours. Think about it. Would you have come if *I* had texted you?"

"What the . . . ?" He frowned and looked at her for a long moment. "*You* texted me? But I don't even—"

"I needed to get you out of your house."

He took a step toward her.

She tightened her grip on the gun and raised it so that it was aimed at his face.

He took a step backward. Toward the bedroom. "Why are you doing this?"

"I didn't want it to come to this, but you kept coming back."

"What are you talking about? You texted me to come here. You just said so yourself."

She motioned to the couch, where she'd placed the knife.

His eyes followed hers and widened.

"What the hell?"

"You haven't asked me why I wanted you out of your house."

Boyd was silent. A litany of emotions played on his face. He was even slower than she'd thought.

"Ask me!" she hissed.

"Why . . . why did you want me out of my house?"

"Because I had business to tend to. With your wife."

The muscles in his jaw flexed. "My wife?"

She watched his eyes slip over the knife again, then quickly return to her. His face darkened. "What did you do?" he asked, his words coming out carefully. "What did you do?" he asked again, even more slowly, as though she were a toddler. As though *she* was the one who didn't get it.

"I slit her throat."

Boyd stared at her. He smiled nervously. "No. There's no way." But then the smile melted, and she watched the muscles in his jaw flex again. "This isn't funny."

"I wasn't going for funny."

"You . . . you don't have it in you," he stammered.

"You'd be surprised."

He sank his fingers into his thick hair, gathered some between his fingers, glanced quickly at the knife again.

"Want to know a fun fact about that knife?"

Elizabeth could see him struggling with the revelation. After a moment, it seemed to register. What she was admitting to.

"You . . . you can't be serious."

"There it is. I just saw the light bulb go on. Finally. There *is* a brain in there, isn't there?"

He glowered at her. "Fuck you."

He snatched the knife from the couch. Brandished it in front of her. She cocked the gun.

"Oops. Poorly played. Now your fingerprints are on it. And when the police find your body with that knife in your hands," she continued, "we can finally put all of this behind us. Put *you* behind us."

He looked down at the knife trembling in his hand.

"I should thank you, Boyd. You made this so easy for me. I was expecting at least a little bit of a challenge."

She calmly squeezed the trigger twice; both shots hit him in the chest.

He crumbled to the Pergo floor.

She walked over to him and looked down.

He looked up at her, holding his chest, blood bubbling up from his shirt, frothy, more pink than red. He blinked a couple of times; then his eyes went still.

She studied him, trying to cement the visual in her mind so she could replay it again later. Then she reached into his coat pocket for his phone. She needed to hide it quickly before the police responded to the gunshots. She couldn't leave any evidence for them to find.

Now to hide his phone. She ejected the battery and was searching for a good place to hide both pieces when she heard Chelsea begin to stir from her slumber.

No, no, no!

It was too soon.

CHAPTER 37

CHELSEA'S EYES POPPED open, the stink of sulfur burning her nostrils. The odor was immediately familiar to her, reminding her of the shooting range.

She walked cautiously in the darkness, trying to get her bearings. Her head was muddy from the pills Elizabeth had given her.

What *had* Elizabeth given her?

Whatever it had been, it must have been strong. Once she pulled herself out of the thick fog, she realized she was standing in the living room. She fumbled for the lamp and flipped it on. Her breath caught.

Boyd was lying motionless in front of her on the carpet.

"Boyd?"

He was lying still. Too still. There was blood on his beige jacket.

A bolt of terror shot through her, quickly sobering her. "Oh, my God! Boyd!"

She fell to her knees.

What . . . what happened?

The room shimmering in front of her eyes, she quickly saw that his chest wasn't rising or falling. She pressed two fingers to his neck and searched for a pulse but found nothing. She tried a second time and got the same result.

Oh, my God.

She peered around. Blood was spattered on one of her yellow throw pillows. Across one of her framed sketches. There was a knife next to Boyd's hand. Then she saw the gun on the floor.

It was *her* gun.

Her heart pounded so hard, she thought it might stop. She tried to piece together the puzzle. But the pills were clouding her mind, making it work too slowly.

She heard Elizabeth's voice behind her. "Thank *God* you're okay."

Chelsea turned to Elizabeth.

Elizabeth! Thank God she was there.

But where had she come from? And how long had she been there?

Hold on. Elizabeth. Had *she* shot Boyd?

"Thank God you had that gun!"

Chelsea frowned.

"Chels, you had no choice," she said, her green eyes earnest. "He was going to kill you."

"Wait. What?" she asked, her tongue thick, heavy.

"He obviously came here to hurt you. What you did was totally self-defense. No one will blame you. You did what you had to do. What you *needed* to do."

Chelsea stared at the gun and then at Boyd's motionless body. Cold dread curled in her chest. Something was very wrong here. More tears spilled down her cheeks. Confused, she shook her head. "But I didn't . . ."

Elizabeth knelt in front of her, pity in her eyes. She placed her hands on Chelsea's shoulders. "It's going to be okay. I'm going to help you get through this. You're going to be just fine."

Chelsea replayed the events in her head the way she'd remembered them. She was groggy, but she knew she'd been asleep. Hadn't she?

Yes. She was certain.

Well, almost.

She replayed everything that had happened since she'd first smelled the sulfur.

She shook her head. She'd never had the gun. She would have remembered it. Remembered something about it at least, like maybe the way it had felt in her hands.

No, she didn't shoot him. She knew she didn't. What Elizabeth was saying wasn't making sense.

Then she had a thought that soothed her a little.

Maybe this is just a dream. A nightmare. Like the others.

She clenched her eyes shut, counted to five, reopened them. But she was still in the living room. Elizabeth's green eyes were still on her, expecting her to say she'd shot Boyd.

"I swear I didn't do this. I never had the gun. I was asleep."

"Oh, Chelsea. You're just not thinking clearly. But it's okay. No one's blaming you. He didn't give you a choice."

Could I have blacked out?

"You blacked out, Chels. You did it while you were blacked out. And you just don't remember."

Chelsea studied Elizabeth's face. Was her left cheek twitching?

Yes. It was.

She was lying.

Why is she lying? Fear turned her insides into ice water. Sirens blaring in her head, she struggled to replay everything she could remember again. She didn't want to be wrong. She *couldn't* be wrong.

She'd smelled sulfur and opened her eyes. When she realized she was in the living room, she'd turned the lamp on and seen Boyd. He was already on the floor, lying motionless. That was exactly what had happened. That was *all* that had happened.

She let her eyes slide over to the gun.

"*You* shot him," she muttered, looking up at Elizabeth.

Elizabeth frowned. "What? No, I didn't. *You* did it."

Chelsea shook her head. "No."

"You took tranquilizers," Elizabeth said, her face pinched with anger. "So you just don't remember."

"You gave me those tranquilizers, Elizabeth."

Elizabeth sprang to her feet and glowered down at her. "Look, you need to just accept what you've done. Before the cops get here."

She felt guilty for questioning Elizabeth. She loved Elizabeth. She depended on Elizabeth. But Elizabeth was lying to her.

"Why are you lying to me?"

The vein in Elizabeth's forehead pulsed. "*You* shot him. It was self-defense. What part of it can you not get through that thick skull of yours? We don't have much time, Chelsea. Quit screwing around."

Elizabeth pinched the bridge of her nose and began pacing. After a moment, she whirled around and faced Chelsea again. Her eyes were smoldering. "Look, I do everything for you. *Everything.* I take care of you. I protect you. I clean up your messes. And what do you do? You go and fuck things up by getting back in touch with Boyd, who I *warned* you to stay away from and then . . . *then* . . . when he comes here to attack you and you kill him in self-defense, you want to blame it on *me*?" She cocked her head and peered at Chelsea. "Just what kind of friend are you?"

Elizabeth had never talked to her like this before. Never. She'd never been angry like this. Not at her. If she believed just one little bit of what Elizabeth had just said, she would have felt awful and would have been quick to apologize. But she *knew* she was right about this.

"You have no clue everything I've done for you," Elizabeth continued. "The *lengths* I've gone just to keep you safe all these years."

Chelsea stared at her in disbelief. So much was wrong suddenly. She felt like her world had completely tilted on its axis.

Elizabeth glared at her. "Now get your story straight because the police will be here soon, and you can't mention me. You *have* to tell them you did it. Because you did."

Elizabeth's cheek twitched again.

A ripple of fear shot through her.

"Please. Tell me what's really going on," she whispered.

"What's *really* going on?" Elizabeth screamed. "I saved your *ass*! I always save your ass!" She leaned in, so close Chelsea could smell her stale breath. "Time and time again. Don't you see? I had to protect you. You're too innocent and fragile to do it for yourself!"

Chelsea continued to stare.

"You *made* me!" Elizabeth screamed. "You've *always* made me!"

You made me.

The words that had been written on the mirror the night of the murders. The same words from the notes.

Elizabeth's face twisted into something awful. But Chelsea didn't look away. She couldn't. Not because she didn't want to, but because she was frozen.

"Jesus! We don't have time for this now!" Elizabeth spat. "Right now we need to get your *goddamn* story together!"

"That night. The message on the mirror. You—"

Elizabeth whirled around.

"Are you not *hearing* me?"

Elizabeth knelt again. She pressed her hands to Chelsea's shoulders, and Chelsea recoiled beneath her touch. "Look, the cops are going to be here any minute. Do you *not* understand how important this is? You can either tell them the truth, that you did this in self-defense. Or you can accuse me. But if you do that . . . if you say that I was here, *even mention me at all*, I will stop protecting you. And they'll know all about your episodes. How screwed up you really are. And you'll go back to the psychiatric hospital for a long time. Trust me."

What is happening?

Elizabeth was supposed to be her friend. Her rock. It had all been a lie. But why?

Chelsea's eyes slid back to Boyd's body. She stared at the dark blood that was congealing across his chest. The blood pooled on the floor around him.

The room began to spin.

She heard Elizabeth moving around the apartment, muttering angrily to herself.

Her head started to pound, and she felt like she was going to vomit. Either *she* was losing it or Elizabeth was. And she didn't know which was worse. She was certain she couldn't get by without Elizabeth. And there was no way she wanted to live if her mind was failing her again.

Her stomach twisted. A few weeks ago, things had been looking up. She'd been so hopeful. Now she'd not only lost Boyd but Elizabeth, and maybe even her mind. She had nothing now. Nothing to live for.

Blood whooshing in her ears, she reached into her bra for the blade. Her heartbeat roared as she removed the cheesecloth and watched it flutter to the carpet. She understood now that, in a way, she'd been waiting for this moment for years.

Her eyes filling with tears, she held her breath and raked the blade hard against the pale skin of her left wrist. She didn't feel any pain, just heat, adrenaline rushing through her.

Blood slowly spilled down her arm, dripped onto the Pergo. As she aimed the blade for her right wrist, the room began to spin again, and everything grew blurry and just a bit darker. She knew what was happening; she was slipping away again. Like she did before her blackouts.

If she was going to do this, finally do this, and do it right, she would need to hurry. She concentrated on her right wrist and again bore down hard on the blade. This time the blood spilled faster, and she felt herself begin to relax.

Her jaw unclenched, then her shoulders. She lay on her side, the floor smooth against her cheek, and felt the knot in her middle start to unfurl. Her wrists throbbed as the blood pulsed from her body.

The room grew darker.

"Chelsea, no!" she heard Elizabeth shriek from somewhere in the distance, just as everything faded to black.

CHAPTER 38

LANG BANGED THE steering wheel impatiently with the heel of his hand as he tried to maneuver through Boston's snarling traffic. Beethoven's Seventh Symphony streamed through the car's speakers as he looked out at Boylston Street jammed with honking cars.

His police light was flashing, but there was no place for any cars to go. Lang weaved on to the shoulder and gunned the engine. He hit Chelsea's number on speed dial again, but just like every other attempt, he was sent right to voice mail. Either she was on the other line or her phone was turned off.

Shit!

He felt an urgency to warn her about Elizabeth. Until he got to the bottom of who she really was, he needed Chelsea to stay away from her.

Lang looked up from his phone, and his eyes widened. He slammed on the brakes and swerved, barely missing a startled pedestrian.

Christ!

Goose bumps broke out along his arms at the near miss. He glanced in his rearview mirror and saw a man waving his fist in the air.

"Shit. Sorry, buddy," he muttered.

As he inched closer to Chelsea's apartment building, he reviewed every inch of the case in his mind again, trying to put the puzzle pieces together. But so many still didn't fit.

First, the evidence against Ethan. What did they have on him that wasn't circumstantial? His semen found inside Christine. His fingerprints on the knife block that the suspected murder weapon had been taken from. The fact that he had disappeared right after the slayings. Yes, Ethan being the perpetrator was certainly plausible—and until now it was the best they'd had to go on. But Lang was all but certain that body in the pond was Ethan's. And it didn't look like he accidentally drove into the pond. So while Ethan still couldn't be ruled out as the murderer, he *could* definitely be ruled out as the one who had been threatening Chelsea with the notes. And if Ethan *hadn't* been the murderer but in fact another victim, the real killer had been much smarter than they'd previously suspected.

Then there was Boyd. Boyd didn't have the makings of a murderer. He was much too anxious. Too afraid of getting caught to taunt Chelsea with notes and threats. He couldn't even lie about an affair without breaking into a sweat.

Even without the airtight alibi, Katherine had never been a viable suspect, although he knew there was more to learn from her. And he planned to. As soon as he found out what was going on with Elizabeth . . . who was now his main focus. Until now, he hadn't been that interested in Elizabeth Jessup. She had been just another *i* to dot and *t* to cross. But the facts that no one by that name ever worked at the psychiatric hospital and that her phone was out of order brought her to the top of his list.

While Elizabeth certainly could have been the person leaving the notes, Chelsea said they hadn't met until after the murders. But with her memory issues, maybe that wasn't true.

But . . . if Elizabeth had been Christine's and Amy's killer, why would she now be Chelsea's closest friend? Could it be guilt? A way to keep tabs on her in case her memory suddenly came rushing back? And what would have been her motive to kill those girls? What was her connection to everyone?

Also, why leave the notes? After five years of nothing? What triggered the need to torment Chelsea?

He needed to speak to Elizabeth.

Immediately.

He quickly parked around the corner from the apartment building. As he was heading into the building, his cell phone rang. He pulled it out of his pocket and looked at the screen. It was Garcia.

"Lang," he answered.

"It's Garcia. Wanted you to know we ran a full check on Elizabeth Jessup. There's no record of her. *Anywhere.* DMV. Police reports. IRS."

Lang's pulse kicked up another notch. "So the name's probably an alias."

"Appears that way."

Lang drew his weapon and gave Garcia his location. He requested backup; then he climbed the stairs to apartment 6D. Once he got there, he knocked on the door loudly and waited.

No answer.

He knocked again.

Again, no answer.

He heard someone on the stairwell. He lowered his weapon and was backing away from the apartment when the door to the stairwell flew open and a man appeared, holding a bag of groceries. Seeing Lang's weapon, the man's eyes widened.

"It's okay. I'm police," Lang said.

"What's going on? Is everything okay?" the man asked.

"Do you know the woman who lives in this unit?" Lang asked, motioning with his chin to apartment 6D.

The man gave him a funny look. "It's vacant. No one's lived there for almost two years now."

Blood surged through Lang's veins. "Are you sure?"

"Yeah. I'm positive."

Lang's heart pounded harder. Something was very wrong. He turned to go back down the stairs. As he hurried toward Chelsea's apartment, he heard shots ring out from somewhere below.

CHAPTER 39

TWO DAYS LATER, Lang knocked lightly on the door of Chelsea's hospital room. She turned her head and gazed at him. Her face looked pale and drawn beneath the fluorescent lighting. A nurse was at her bedside taking her blood pressure.

Lang had found her in her apartment out cold, both wrists slashed, lying on the floor, close to Boyd Lawson's body. Since she'd been rushed to the hospital, he'd visited twice, but both times she'd been sedated heavily and sleeping. Luckily, Garcia had been able to speak with her last night.

Garcia told Lang that Chelsea reported she'd let Boyd into her apartment, and he'd tried to attack her with a knife. Garcia said so far, it appeared to be a clear case of self-defense.

Lang pushed the door open and smiled at Chelsea. "I hear you're staying another day or two for observation?"

Chelsea blinked at him, her face expressionless.

The nurse greeted him and stepped out of the room.

Lang walked closer to Chelsea and held out the bouquet of lilies he'd bought at the gift shop downstairs. "I brought you a little something."

Chelsea's nod was nearly imperceptible.

He set the lilies on her table tray, then turned back to her. "I'm glad you're okay," he said softly.

"Thanks."

"Are you up to talking a little?"

"Sure," she said, her voice deeper than usual, hoarse.

"We found Ethan's body. He was in his car at the bottom of a pond back in Springfield."

Chelsea's eyes flickered.

"It was on the same property as a set of your foster parents. The ones I had asked you about last week. John and Delores Jones."

Her eyes seemed to flash; then she looked away, in the direction of the room's only window.

Lang continued. "So, both Boyd and Ethan are gone now. You should feel safer."

She nodded.

Lang had expected her to be upset, confused, maybe angry—and to certainly have a lot of questions. He was surprised by her reactions, or lack of them. Maybe it was the sedative. Maybe she'd gotten more of it this morning. He should have stopped by the nurses' station to find out before visiting.

Her reaction could also be a product of him overloading her with information. That on top of the trauma she was surely suffering from killing someone. Whether it was self-defense or not, taking a human life was always very difficult on the psyche.

"Are you okay?" he asked.

"Yes."

"Do you need time to let that soak in before I go on?"

"No. I'm fine."

"Okay. So, there are a few loose ends that are still troubling me," he started. "Things that I need to look into immediately, that I'm hoping you can help me with."

Her eyes were on him again.

"Your friend Elizabeth. Have you heard from her?"

Her cheek twitched a little. "No."

"The apartment number you gave me: Six D. Are you sure that's the right apartment?"

Chelsea nodded.

"Have you been to that apartment?"

Chelsea seemed to struggle to think. Finally, she shook her head. "I guess I never have. She always came down to my place."

"Really? And you didn't find that odd?"

Chelsea seemed to grow paler. "Yeah, maybe. Now that I'm saying it out loud. Yes, I guess it is."

"The phone number you gave me. It's not working."

"That's . . . strange."

"Do you have any other contact information for her?"

She shook her head.

"And you're sure you gave me the right phone number?"

He showed her the number written in his notebook. She studied it and nodded slowly.

"Yes."

She swung her legs to the side of the bed, grabbed the back of her hospital gown with one hand, and tried to steady herself with the other.

"Do you need something?" Lang asked, holding out a hand to help steady her.

"I need to use the bathroom."

Lang helped her walk to the small bathroom. He watched as she shut the door. A moment later he heard the faucet turn on inside, followed by the muffled sound of vomiting.

"Do you need any help?" he called after she'd finished. "Should I get the nurse?"

"No, I'm okay," she said weakly from the other side of the door.

Lang hadn't meant to cause her any more distress. Still, he needed the information. He thought about the fact that she'd never been to Elizabeth's apartment. The fact that there was no record of her.

His cell phone rang. He looked at the screen. McCutcheon, the FBI agent in charge of recovering data from the phone that had been found in the Joneses' pond. So far they had been able to trace the phone back to its owner, one of the deceased girls, Amy Harris. The memory chip was corroded from being submerged for so long, so he wasn't sure what they would be able to recover from it, if anything. But he'd been hopeful. This call could be important.

"I have to take a call," he said through the door. "I'll be right back."

He ducked out of Chelsea's room. "Lang here," he said.

"Lang, this is Agent McCutcheon. I work out of the Springfield FBI field off—"

The call dropped.

"Shit," he muttered.

He limped through the corridor, looking for a place where he could get better reception. But the most he seemed to be able to get on Chelsea's floor was one bar. He waited on an elevator and took it to the first floor, then crossed the lobby as quickly as he could and exited the double doors of the hospital.

He had four bars now.

A new text message came through from McCutcheon with a video file attached.

The text read: Bingo! Our tech guy discovered Amy Harris had a MobileMe account back in 2010 when mobile data backup was still in its infancy. Law enforcement hadn't yet been trained on the technology, so chances are Duplechaine and his tech guys wouldn't have even known to look for it. Check out the attached. Harris was recording a video the night when all hell broke loose.

The thumbnail photo was of Amy Harris.

Lang's pulse quickened, and he pressed "Play."

In the clip, redheaded Amy was alive and well, lying on her stomach on her bed. She was propped up on her elbows, her eyes heavily made up. The phone was about a foot or so in front of her and situated on something stable. Remembering the location of the furniture in her bedroom, Lang guessed it had been her dresser.

The video came to life, and Lang could hear Amy talking excitedly. "Well, I guess that's all for tonight. Like I said, I hadn't planned on making this video tonight but figured you'd like to know how my Halloween birthday went!" she said, her words a little warbled, her eyes glazed, probably from all the alcohol and Ecstasy that had been found in her system. "Look for a new video on Monday. I'll be unboxing my latest MAC order, and I'll show you how to . . ." Amy frowned, and her head swiveled toward her bedroom door.

He watched her sit up on her knees and say something to someone. Lang heard something that sounded like it could be a scream in the background. "Christine?" Amy called. "What's—"

Another sound in the distance. Definitely a scream.

Amy's frown deepened. "Christine?" she called again.

Silence.

Amy crawled off the bed and moved toward the door, out of the frame. "Christine? What's going on?" Lang heard her say softly.

Suddenly, Amy was struggling with someone, just out of the frame. He could see a flurry of arms. "No! Please!" she pleaded. "Why . . . are you—"

Then he heard another voice. It was a female voice, muffled. She said something Lang couldn't make out. Amy screamed again and then was partially back in the frame. All he could see were arms and hair and the glint of a knife's blade. The other girl appeared in the frame. She had long, dark hair. But the angle was wrong, and he couldn't see her face.

Both girls were on the bed now, struggling. The unidentified girl had Amy pinned to the bed. He couldn't see the knife. Someone was saying something. It was the brunette. Lang leaned in, trying to make it out. "Beg me to stop."

Amy pleaded. "Please."

"No. Say, 'Please, Elizabeth. Stop.'"

Chelsea's friend Elizabeth.

"Bingo," Lang muttered in excitement.

But how the hell did Elizabeth, a nurse Chelsea said she'd met at the hospital only after the killings, fit into this puzzle?

The knife was suddenly back. He heard Amy scream. Something must have hit the dresser because the video image shifted. Amy and her attacker were out of view again.

Lang strained to make out what he could. Amy let out another noise, a faint, weaker attempt at a scream.

The angle of the video moved yet again, bumping the two women partially back into view. Then something caught Lang's attention. As though reading his mind, the image on the screen froze.

Lang looked closely.

Against the back wall was a mirror, and the reflection of the killer's face appeared. But it was too distant. He squinted, not able to make out enough. It wasn't going to be enough to get a positive ID.

His phone rang. McCutcheon again. But Lang needed to see the rest of the video. There were only twenty seconds left. He'd call McCutcheon back when he was done.

It looked like the video had been altered. Edited, perhaps by McCutcheon and his team. The pixelated image sharpened. This time, the woman's features were much clearer. Clear enough for an identification.

The hair on his arms stood up.

He shook his head. *Oh, no. No. Shit!*

It was Chelsea.

"Shit, shit, *shit!*"

An elderly woman in a wheelchair stared at him.

Just as he was about to press Garcia on his speed dial, his phone rang again. It was Garcia. "Lang," he answered, breathless, limping through the double doors of the hospital. He had to get back up to Chelsea's room as quickly as he could, but he needed backup.

"See the video?" Garcia asked.

"Yeah, just did. Where are you?"

He heard police sirens in the distance. "Half a block away."

"I'm about to be in an elevator," Lang said. "Heading to her room now."

"We'll be right there," Garcia said.

Lang heard a click.

He rode the elevator up, his heart jogging in his chest. He exited on the sixth floor and limped through the ward, back to Chelsea's hospital room. When he got there, Chelsea's bed was empty. The bathroom, too.

A nurse looked curiously on.

"Anyone see Chelsea Dutton?" he barked.

Looking surprised by his urgency, the nurse shook her head.

He hurried to the nurses' station and asked if anyone had any knowledge of her whereabouts.

But they didn't. No one had seen her leave her room.

A security guard came running toward him. Garcia's team must have already placed a call to the hospital's watch commander. "Put someone on all the exits to this hospital, stat!" Lang commanded.

"Will do, sir," the guard said and lowered his head, giving orders in his walkie-talkie.

Lang's heart dropped and landed with a thud in his stomach. He shook his head.

Chelsea was gone.

CHAPTER 40

LANG PUSHED OPEN the door to the Springfield police station. It had been almost twenty-four hours since he'd seen Chelsea in the hospital, and he was still feeling gutted that she'd been the killer all along.

There were so many unanswered questions. The most important ones: Why had she called herself Elizabeth? And did her mystery friend, Elizabeth Jessup, even exist?

He'd watched the camera footage of her exiting the hospital via the freight entrance eight hours after the search had commenced. She'd gotten ahold of a pair of scrubs and a lanyard and could be seen walking out nonchalantly. There was an APB out on her. Her apartment was also being monitored, as well as her vehicle, credit cards, and cell phone.

He'd received permission to assemble a task force and had just left the second meeting. Several cops were out searching for her, and calls to the tip line were flooding in and being verified. So far they knew that she'd used an Uber to drive her from a coffee shop six blocks from the hospital to a post office on Hudson Street. The driver had said she'd stayed in there for less than five minutes, then had him drive her to South Station. Surveillance footage at South Station confirmed she was there, and a clerk working for Greyhound confirmed she'd paid cash for a ticket to Roanoke, Virginia. They also had reason to believe that from Roanoke, she might have gone on to Florida. Lang had guys working on verifying that now. If they confirmed she was indeed headed to Florida, he was catching a red-eye there tonight.

But this afternoon he had appointments to talk with Katherine Jones and Dr. Swenson. Lang now limped down the hall, the click of his brown loafers echoing off the polished tile floor, and entered the last interview room. Katherine was sitting at the single gray table that was anchored in the middle of the room. She sat with her spine straight, her hands folded in her lap, like a student waiting to speak to the school's principal. She hadn't brought her lawyer this time. She was alone.

The room was stark and dreary. Two surveillance cameras were positioned on opposite walls above a large two-way mirror. Other than the gray table and two metal chairs, the room was empty.

Lang walked in and nodded at her.

"Would you like anything to drink? Coffee? Water?"

She shook her head.

He sat down and could see she had been crying. "Thank you for meeting me."

Katherine nodded. "I already gave my statement."

"Yes. I know."

"I have no idea how that car . . . that boy . . . ended up on my parents' property. I wasn't even in the country when the murders happened."

"We know. You were overseas."

"Then why . . ."

Lang pulled a folder out of the brown leather briefcase he'd brought with him.

"I need to know why you lied about visiting Chelsea after the murders."

Lang slid a copy of the visitor log in front of Katherine.

Katherine's face flushed.

"This record shows you visited her in the hospital a week after the murders."

Katherine stared at the photocopied log for a long time, her face void of expression.

Lang studied her.

Was she deciding to tell the truth, or busy formulating a new lie?

She looked up. "I'm sorry I wasn't exactly honest about—"

"You weren't not 'exactly honest,' Katherine. Let's call it like it is. You lied. You lied, and you wasted my time."

She blinked. "Yes, you're right. I did lie. I just didn't want to get involved. I wanted to tell you what I knew. Then I wanted you to go away."

"Because you had a dead kid on your property? Decomposing at the bottom of your pond?"

Her eyes glistened. "I swear to you—I didn't know anything about him. My God, I feel sick every time I think about that poor boy. Him being down there, all those years. I had *no* idea. I work my ass off on those textbooks and never go back there. No one goes back there. Ever. There's no reason for anyone to."

Lang reached for the box of tissues and slid it toward her.

"So, why did you visit her?"

Katherine grabbed a tissue and dabbed her eyes.

"I visited her because I felt guilty for getting her into some trouble when she lived with my parents. I wanted to see if I could bring her anything, help her in some way while she was in the hospital."

"Tell me about the trouble you got her into."

She looked down at her hands, then back up at him. "One time I stole twenty dollars from my father's wallet, and when he noticed, I lied and said she was the one who did it. I knew it was wrong, but I was young and stupid, and I had no idea it would turn into such a big deal. The lie ended up snowballing out of control."

Lang listened.

"When my parents asked her why she took the money, she said she didn't do it. That I was lying. My parents believed me over her, and that made her very angry. Like *really* angry. It shocked my parents how angry she could be, so they talked to DCF, who told them to bring her to a psychiatrist. Before I knew it, they started talking about sending her back to DCF. I still feel bad for doing that to her. I had no idea that would happen when I did it. I was just immature, and she creeped me out, so I didn't think twice about pinning it on her at the time. I didn't visit her again after that. And I didn't see how telling you any of that could help your investigation."

"You said she creeped you out. Why?"

Katherine shrugged. "She just scared me. She wasn't mean or malicious or anything. She was just really quiet. But in a weird way. The only time she talked was to that imaginary friend of hers when she thought she was alone."

"Imaginary friend?"

"Yeah. She talked to her all the time."

"Did her imaginary friend have a name?"

Katherine nodded. "Yeah, Elizabeth. She called her Elizabeth."

CHAPTER 41

AN HOUR LATER, Lang sat in Dr. Swenson's cramped office, which was housed in a small medical-office building in Chicopee, just outside Springfield. Dr. Swenson was the psychiatrist who had treated Chelsea when she'd lived with the Jones family. Per Delores Jones's notes, Chelsea's last appointment with him had created quite an upheaval. Lang wanted to know why.

He'd been waiting for about five minutes when Dr. Swenson walked hastily into the room. "Sorry for the wait." Swenson went to a cabinet and fished out a file, then sat down behind his sturdy mahogany desk. "I'm also sorry it took me so long to return your messages."

"Not a problem," Lang said. He stood and handed Swenson the subpoena that allowed Swenson to talk about Chelsea's case. He watched the doctor stroke his salt-and-pepper beard while he read through it. Then Lang brought him up to date, telling him about the Springfield Coed Killings. About Chelsea being wounded. The notes and subsequent shooting of Boyd, along with her own suicide attempt. Finally, he told him about the discovery on the video and the fact that she was now at large.

When he finished, Swenson was frowning. He shook his head. "I remember hearing about those murders when I was in Florida, but I didn't know Miss Dutton was a part of that. And no one knows where she is now?"

"Not yet, but there are a lot of uniforms out there looking for her. So hopefully it's just a matter of time."

Swenson shook his head again. "I'm very sorry to hear about this. It's truly awful."

Lang nodded his agreement.

"So, what exactly is it I can help you with, Detective Lang?"

"I found some notes from Delores Jones—Chelsea's foster mother at the time you were seeing her as a patient. She said you made a diagnosis that troubled them. I was hoping you could tell me what that diagnosis was. It wasn't in any of the files."

"Well, it was more of an assessment than an official diagnosis. I only had six sessions with her," Swenson said. "But it was more than enough to see that Chelsea was a special case. One that would be better diagnosed and treated by a different doctor. One with experience with cases like hers.

"I told Mrs. Jones as much. I advised her to send Chelsea to Dr. Jacob Tannon in Boston. At the time, he'd already worked with many cases like Chelsea's. And I knew he'd be able to better help her." He paused. "By chance, do you know if Mrs. Jones followed up on my recommendation?"

"I'm guessing not. Two nights after Chelsea's last visit with you, the Joneses' home caught fire. Delores and her husband were asleep in the house at the time. They didn't survive."

Swenson closed his eyes. "Oh, dear God. I'm sorry to hear that."

"You said you made an assessment of Chelsea Dutton. Can you explain?"

"Of course. I had speculated that Chelsea suffered from dissociative identity disorder."

Lang frowned and shook his head.

"You may know it by a more blanket term—multiple personality disorder."

"Different people living in one body?"

"In a manner of speaking, yes, but it's more complicated than that."

Lang had no idea that was even a real diagnosis.

"DID is far more common than multiple personality disorder, actually. It affects millions of people around the world. It happens mostly in young children as a kind of protective mechanism. The personality ends up fragmenting to protect a centralized 'me,' if you will. This personality doesn't always have control over—or even know about—the other personalities."

Lang thought about the imaginary friend Katherine had told him about: Elizabeth.

"So, you're saying Chelsea had this?"

"Yes. I believed her to. But like I said, that sort of diagnosis is a bit out of my league."

"But I've spoken to Chelsea Dutton several times. How could someone have this condition and it go unnoticed?"

"DID is very good at hiding. It does not want to be found. Many people don't get diagnoses or even suspect it until they're well into middle age. And some people go their whole lifetimes undiagnosed, not even realizing they have it."

"She just switches back and forth between personalities?"

"Not always at will. And I don't believe it was in Miss Dutton's case."

Dr. Swenson threaded his fingers together and set his hands on his desk. "From what I observed, there are two very distinct personalities. The gentle, well-behaved, but very vulnerable, Chelsea. And the aggressive—and from what you've told me, maybe even psychopathic—protector personality, Elizabeth."

Lang sank deeper into his seat, trying to wrap his head around the strange concept. "You're saying that Chelsea has been hiding Elizabeth this entire time?"

"Oh, Chelsea probably isn't hiding her. That's the thing. The host personality is usually unaware of other personalities. She's most likely unaware that Elizabeth isn't real. When Mrs. Jones brought Chelsea in to see me, it was very clear to me that Elizabeth was aware of Chelsea as the host personality. But not vice versa."

Lang was confused. "But Chelsea knew about Elizabeth. She said she was her friend. That they met at the hospital, and they lived in the same apartment building. Chelsea gave me Elizabeth's phone number and apartment number. But both were fake."

Dr. Swenson nodded. "Sometimes to justify the existence of another personality, a dominant personality will subconsciously create an entire life for it. They may see the other personality as an actual person."

Lang remembered how Chelsea never struck him as dishonest. He had never glimpsed even the remotest hint of deceit. But if she had another personality—and thought that person was real—then, in her mind, she hadn't been lying.

Dr. Swenson nodded. "I know. It's a lot to digest."

Lang nodded. "So why would Chelsea try to slit her wrists after going through all that work to kill Boyd Lawson?"

Dr. Swenson took off his glasses, set them on his desk. "Again, just conjecture, but it might not have been Chelsea who killed him. It might have been Elizabeth. It's possible that after everything she's been through, Chelsea's brain couldn't take the additional emotional trauma." He leaned forward. "I will say this, though: Of the types of personalities that would resort to suicide, Chelsea is at greatest risk."

Lang slowly processed the information Dr. Swenson was giving him.

"The woman I saw in the hospital the other day. She didn't seem like Chelsea at all. Do you think she could have been Elizabeth then? Just playing along?"

"Perhaps, but—and here's another place where it's purely hypothetical—it's rare for one personality to impersonate the other. Unless . . ."

"Unless what?"

"Unless Chelsea's personality really did die . . . or at least became silenced when she slit her wrists."

Lang furrowed his brow, again confused.

"At that point, Elizabeth, the subordinate personality, could have become the dominant one—possibly even taking over completely. It's not common, but it has been known to happen."

"So, you're saying that there's a possibility that Chelsea's personality is dead?"

"Yes. It's a possibility."

"Now the person walking around somewhere out there . . . she could be Elizabeth?"

"Yes. But let's hope that's not the case."

"Why do you say that?"

"Because Chelsea served as the conscience in their dualistic personalities. The healthy, caring yin to Elizabeth's sociopathic yang. Without that stopgap, Elizabeth will go unchecked. And from what we've both seen, she appears to be a very dangerous woman."

CHAPTER 42

BACK AT THE motel, Lang finished packing. He was taking a red-eye from Logan International to Miami International. There'd been several sightings of Chelsea in the area, and he wanted to meet with their FBI field office.

"You're saying Elizabeth might have committed those murders and Chelsea might not even know about them?" Janie asked, folding one of his shirts and placing it in his suitcase.

"From what Swenson told me, it's definitely a possibility."

"God, the things she's been through in her short life. I feel horrible for the poor girl."

"Me, too."

Lang got a lump in his throat. He'd wanted good things for Chelsea. He'd been rooting for her. And now she might be dead, so to speak. As though sensing Lang was thinking about his owner, Harry jumped up on the bed and meowed. Lang pet the cat for a moment, then grabbed his carrier. He knew Chelsea had loved the cat, and he hadn't had the heart to let Garcia's officer take Harry to the pound. Janie had agreed to bring him to Victoria. They'd provide a good home for him, and Nicky would get that surprise he'd asked for.

They left the motel and headed for Logan. As he drove, Lang sighed. He was still having a difficult time with everything he'd learned. He wanted nothing more in this moment than to help Chelsea. He realized the best thing he could do was catch up with Elizabeth and take her into custody. And that was what he was going to do.

He was as determined as ever.

Lang wondered where Elizabeth was tonight. Now that he knew whom he was really looking for, it was a matter of when he would find her, not if.

As he pulled in to the passenger drop-off area, he let his thoughts wander back to everything Dr. Swenson had shared with him. The power of the mind and how it protected itself. He'd been protecting his mind, too. With Janie. Victoria was right. Janie was a gift not to be taken for granted. He knew that most men would never find a Janie during their lifetimes. He had to stop protecting himself. He had to stop waiting for the perfect time to start living his life, because there wasn't going to *be* a perfect time. There never was . . . for anything. He needed to start living in the now.

Standing next to the car, Lang stared into Janie's brown, almond-shaped eyes and pushed a few strands of her blonde hair behind her ear. He studied the crinkling around her eyes. The same crinkling he saw every morning when he looked in the mirror.

God, at the age of forty, she was still a stunner.

Possibly more than she had been seven years ago when they'd first met. She was also very wise. In his younger years, he had no idea he'd find that kind of wisdom so attractive. "Things are going to be different when I get back, okay?"

"Yeah? How so?"

"You'll see. We'll have a long talk. Figure some things out."

"Well, that's a bit cryptic."

"Trust me, okay?"

She smiled. "I do."

A jet flew overhead, its engines splitting the night sky, and he kissed her goodbye.

CHAPTER 43

ELIZABETH APPLIED HER makeup in the hotel mirror.

Just outside her window, crystal-blue waters gently lapped the white sands of Key Largo. Canvas lounging chairs, hammocks, and palm trees dotted the beachfront, along with a dozen or so hotel guests. Mostly baby boomers, quite a few of them divorcées with money, sat drinking and talking loudly at a twenty-foot-long ocean bar.

But she didn't hear any of it.

She was inside her head, remembering that Halloween night five years ago.

After seeing a shit-faced Ethan and Christine beginning to flirt, Elizabeth reached up and took over. Hatred flooded her middle as she sat on the couch, observing. Ethan was with Chelsea, and Christine knew it.

Pretending to be asleep, she quietly watched Ethan kiss Christine, then gather her in his arms and walk back to her bedroom. A minute later, thinking she was asleep, Amy retreated, too, to her own bedroom.

All alone, Elizabeth sprang off the couch and paced the living room. They were disrespecting Chelsea. What Ethan was doing was so wrong.

What Christine was doing was wrong. He was a downright cheat. And she was a whore.

And Elizabeth was going to make them both pay.

She noticed the knife Ethan had used to slice Amy's birthday cake sitting on the coffee table. She picked it up and curled her fingers around the handle.

Ethan and Christine grunted and moaned in Christine's bedroom. A headboard smacked hard against a wall.

Think, think.

Come up with a plan.

A few minutes later, a door clicked in the hallway. Elizabeth heard footsteps, then a door open and close. Pipes clanked in a wall, and she heard the pounding water of the shower.

Elizabeth was plotting when Ethan suddenly appeared. His eyes just slits, it was clear he was drunk or high. If not both. With a lopsided grin, he plopped down on the couch and laid his head in her lap, reeking of sweat and sex. He was so out of it, he hadn't even noticed the knife in her hand.

"I'm so hungry," he muttered. "I could really go for a taco right now."

She stared at him. His mussed hair, his sweaty scalp. She fought the urge to stab him right then and there. She knew that would be too dangerous.

She waited until his breathing became deep, rhythmic. Then she slid out from beneath him. Knife in hand, she stood in front of him and tried to figure out what to do. Just knowing she had the power to kill him right then and there was exhilarating, powerful. The feeling was so intense, she shook.

It was the same feeling she'd had the night she'd set the fire at the Joneses' farm. That had been her first major victory. Her very first taste of killing, and it had been sweet. She and Chelsea had both trusted the

Joneses. Even loved them. But they had been going to send them back into the foster system.

So the couple had gotten what they deserved.

After so many years of being on the receiving end of misplaced power, Elizabeth had found that setting fire to their house, then finding out they hadn't made it out extremely pleasurable. And now she was going to get to do it again.

She heard a noise. She looked up and saw Christine, wrapped in a towel. Her blue eyes bounced between the knife and Elizabeth's face and grew so wide, they looked like they might pop out of her head.

"Chelsea? What are you . . . ," she asked, her voice quivering. Her towel fell away, and she darted down the hallway.

Elizabeth darted after her. Just before Elizabeth could catch up, the girl ducked inside her bedroom and slammed the door. Elizabeth tried to open it, but it was locked. She threw her body into it, but it didn't budge. Elizabeth got a running start and threw her body into it harder. This time it swung open, and she crashed to the floor next to Christine, who had been hurriedly sliding her jeans up over her legs.

Getting a better grip on the knife, Elizabeth jumped to her feet and lunged for Christine's back, but the knife sank into her shoulder instead. Christine screamed out in pain. She thrashed, windmilling her arms and catching Elizabeth in the throat. Elizabeth stumbled back and watched Christine run for the hallway. But Elizabeth caught up to her midway and sank the blade into her once more, this time getting her square between the shoulder blades.

She thought about how easily the blade carved through flesh. It was like semisoft ice cream, Jell-O even. She hadn't expected that.

Christine screamed again, took a few steps, then fell like a sack of potatoes on the living-room floor. When Elizabeth caught up with her again, Christine tried to fight back, but she was too weak.

"Christine?" Amy called from her room.

Elizabeth sprang up.

"Christine? What's going on?"

Elizabeth hurried toward Amy's room. She didn't want to do this. She'd always liked Amy. Amy had been very nice to Chelsea. She hadn't done anything wrong. But Elizabeth didn't have a choice. It was either Amy or them.

Amy appeared in the doorway, and Elizabeth lunged.

A few minutes later, Elizabeth, her shirt glued to her back from sweat and her heart thudding in her ears, returned to the living room. Ethan, still passed out cold, was snoring.

How could he not wake up through all the noise and activity?

He was worthless.

And she was going to treat him that way.

As she wiped the sweat from her forehead, an idea took shape in her mind. She carefully placed the knife on the coffee table, then went to the kitchen. Looking under the sink, she found what she needed.

Rat poison.

Amy had bought it hoping to kill a mouse they'd all seen running around the apartment. Elizabeth had watched enough true-crime shows to know that rat poison contained strychnine, which was fatal to humans. She also knew it tasted sweet, so she hoped it would be undetectable.

She poured some of it into a plastic cup, then poured some Diet Coke and Jack Daniel's over it. She stirred it until it was well blended.

Then she set the drink on the coffee table, along with the knife, and went into Christine's and Amy's rooms, careful not to step in any of the blood spatter. Looking around, she picked up anything that could be incriminating, including Amy's phone, which lay on its side on the dresser. Amy was always making YouTube videos, so God knew what was on there. She threw everything into a plastic shopping bag and set the bag next to the cup.

Then she walked back to the couch. "Wake up," she demanded. "Let's get some food."

Ethan didn't move.

She kicked his leg. Nothing. She tried to shake him. She slapped his face. He still didn't move. So she kicked him, hard, in the ribs. He grabbed his side and rolled off the couch, onto the floor.

His eyes wide but bleary, he stared at her. "What the—"

"I'm hungry. Let's get some tacos. My treat."

He blinked and continued to hold his side. "Tacos. Yeah, sure."

"I'll drive," she said, dangling the keys to his Lexus in front of his face.

"Okay."

Ethan found his shoes and jacket, slipped them on, then stumbled down the hall toward the door. Elizabeth hurried him out to the car.

He plunked down in the passenger seat and motioned to the cup in her hand. "What's that?"

She handed it to him. "A drink for the road. I made it special."

After walking around to the driver's side and getting in, she turned over the ignition and glanced up to see Ethan taking a swig of the drink. He winced. "Jesus, this is strong."

"What? Can't handle it?"

"Dude, I wasn't complaining. I was just surprised is all," he slurred. He flashed her a wide, tired smile, then drank more in silence.

She had just pulled onto Main Street when she heard the cup tumble from his hand and strike the dashboard. He'd passed out.

She stiffened when she passed the turn for Taco Havana and glanced nervously over at him, hoping he hadn't noticed. But he was still passed out, his mouth hanging open.

A minute later, she took a right turn on an uneven country road, and they bounced toward their destination. She had driven out here twice since the fire, and both times the property had been abandoned. She hoped that was still the case.

When they came to a clearing, she realized she was in luck. The place looked just as deserted as ever. The Lexus's headlights shone on the charred foundation where the farmhouse had once been. She passed it, then the barn, then the old trailer.

She kept driving until she got to the far side of the pond, where it was deepest. Once there, she parked the Lexus on the steep embankment and glanced at Ethan. As though he felt her gaze, his eyes popped open.

"Oh, God, I . . . ," he suddenly murmured. He grabbed his throat.

Shit!

Ethan held his stomach, moaning loudly.

She tentatively turned the overhead light on and saw that Ethan's face was green.

"Something's wrong. I—"

He started to spasm. His neck, his shoulders. Then he arched his back. A guttural sound came from his throat, and his back arched again. He grabbed his throat with both hands, then vomited. The noises, the odor of the vomit, made her feel sick.

Her heart pounding, she climbed out of the car and threw all the evidence into the pond, one item at a time. An owl hooted in the distance, and she almost jumped out of her skin. After the last item had splashed its way in, she threw the driver's door open again, lowered the window, and slammed the door shut. Then she crawled back through the open window and slid the car into neutral. She wriggled out of the car as it started its slow descent toward the dark water.

Adrenaline whooshed through her veins as the Lexus crept slowly into the pond. She could hear Ethan still making those awful noises as it sank. Her skin crawled as she waited, expecting at any minute he would jump out of the car. But he didn't. Once the car was completely submerged, she fully expected him to rise from the murky water like the bad guys did in horror movies.

But he didn't.

She watched for several more minutes, until the water stopped bubbling and the surface became calm, peaceful again.

Oh, my God, it actually worked.

The owl hooted again. This time she flipped it the bird, then plunged her hands deep into her pockets and started on the long, freezing walk back to the apartment. She still had several hours before daylight, but every moment counted.

There was more to do.

And the hard part hadn't even begun.

❀ ❀ ❀

A little over an hour later, Elizabeth arrived back at the apartment. She slunk in and looked around, then exhaled with relief.

All was quiet.

The girls were just as she'd left them: Christine lying on the living-room floor. Amy on her bed.

Elizabeth's hands were so cold from the walk, they felt like inanimate objects. Her face was so frigid, she felt it might fall off. She went to the bathroom sink and ran hot water over her freezing hands and tried to think of where she should hide the knife. She thought of possibilities and crossed them out in her head as she stared at her reflection in the mirror.

Her eyes were wide and wild, her hair disheveled and windblown. She smiled at her image, and even to herself, she thought she looked crazy.

Then she had an idea.

She turned and looked down at the floor.

The air vent.

She hurried to the coffee table and grabbed the knife, then returned to the bathroom to see if it would fit.

It did. But just barely.

She went to the junk drawer in the kitchen and grabbed a red marker, then returned to the bathroom and scribbled on the mirror:

YOU MADE ME

It was a message for Chelsea. A double entendre.

She returned the marker to the kitchen. Then, picking up the knife again, she opened both the living-room and bathroom windows and took a big breath. This would be the hardest part. She'd always had a very strong will and an abnormally high tolerance for pain, and she hoped she could pull this off in a believable way.

Her blood electric, she squeezed her eyes shut, held her breath, then raked the blade across the back of her hand. Immediately, beads of blood bubbled up on her knuckles.

She was pleased that she'd felt more adrenaline than pain. But she'd only just gotten started.

Tears pricking her eyes, she pressed the blade hard from her nose to her ear and sliced. Again, the stinging was sharp but tolerable. The blood ran down her cheek and dripped on the carpet.

So far, so good.

She sliced at her arms, each slice a little deeper than the one before it, and walked backward slowly toward the bathroom. She started to feel queasy again. But she didn't stop. It was time for more convincing wounds.

Biting down on her bottom lip, she sank the knife into her left quadriceps and screamed. She quickly sank the knife into the other leg. Blood was really flowing. She tried to not think, to just act, and aimed for the side of her abdomen. The blade went in far too easily, and way too deep, and she screamed out again at the searing pain that seemed to radiate from everywhere. Her eyes flooded with tears.

Shit, oh fuck!

Barely able to breathe, she stumbled her way to the bathroom and turned on the faucet. She rinsed off the knife, then shoved it in the air vent in the floor.

She used toilet paper and quickly cleaned blood from around the vent and flushed the bloody paper down the toilet. Then she stumbled back toward the tub.

She howled in agony as she lifted a leg over the side of the tub, then tried to lift the other leg. She screamed out as loud as she could for help, her mouth aimed at the bathroom window almost three feet above her. The pain was so sharp and hot. She'd had no idea pain could be this bad.

She bent over and vomited. Then she screamed some more. Over and over, hoping someone wouldn't only hear but would also do something about it. Either that, or that she'd quickly die. Her body felt like one giant open sore. It burned and throbbed, and the pain was incredible. Through her tears, she stared at the blood on the tub's porcelain bottom. There was too much.

Clearly, she'd overdone it.

She was losing blood fast, too fast.

The walls started closing in on her. She stumbled, then went down hard. Her head smashed against the tub's edge. Then everything went black.

❁ ❁ ❁

When she'd awakened, she'd learned she'd gotten away with it, just like she had the time before with the Joneses. Real-life cops and CSIs, she had come to realize, weren't as thorough as they appeared in the movies or on television. They were understaffed, overworked, burned out. Their budgets were continually slashed. As a result, they often missed things. Sometimes several things.

During the stay in the psychiatric hospital, Elizabeth had been taken back to the apartment to pack a few personal belongings. The first thing she had done upon returning was retrieve the knife from the vent. She'd stuffed it into an old backpack, and no one had been the wiser.

And, of course, Chelsea hadn't a clue what had happened. Yes, she'd tried to put the puzzle together, but she'd been missing too many pieces.

Chelsea. The thought of Chelsea brought her back to the present, and Elizabeth felt a pang of remorse. Chelsea was gone now. Well, not so much gone as pushed way, way down. So far down, she no longer had a voice.

She'd miss Chelsea. She'd always genuinely cared about her and had done everything possible to ensure her happiness and safety. But this time, Chelsea had given her no other choice. Elizabeth had tried to warn her. She'd told her outright that reconnecting with Boyd was bad news. She'd warned her with the notes. She had been the one who had thrown away those sketches of the Joneses' place, knowing how dangerous they could potentially be if Lang saw them.

Protecting Chelsea had been so much easier when she was younger. As Chelsea had grown older, she'd become more aware, asked more questions, had suddenly wanted friends—all of which posed major challenges for Elizabeth as she'd tried to prevent others from catching on. It had finally become impossible.

Now she didn't have to work so hard to keep it all together. Now *she* was in charge. It was freeing not to have to worry about her anymore.

With her makeup applied, Elizabeth straightened her spine and looked at herself. She'd dyed her hair blonde and cut it into an angular-style bob.

She looked good, like a brand-new woman.

"Hi, I'm Delilah Anderson," she mouthed in the mirror, trying out the name on her fake ID. She decided she looked believable.

She knew that Lang would be coming after her, so she would have to work fast. Either find some lonely man with a yacht who could sail her away to a Caribbean island or jump to the southern Keys. Whatever she did, she couldn't stay in any one place very long.

She grabbed the "Do Not Disturb" sign and slipped it on the doorknob. It was time to mix with the crowd outside.

Chelsea had had her turn.

Now it was hers.

ACKNOWLEDGMENTS

People often say that raising a child takes a village, and I know that was true for me with my twin sons. I have no clue how we would have done it without our village. And we were blessed to have an amazing one.

Writing a novel also takes a village. At least, when I'm the one writing it. I'm so very grateful for those who helped me during the writing of this one, and there were a lot of you!

First and foremost, a huge thank-you to my husband, Brian, who played Mr. Mom again while I worked day and night for many months on this book. A big thank-you to David Wilson for all his amazing help during the writing of this book.

Thanks to Mom and Terry for always being there when I need anything. Sage Gallegos for emotional support and letting me use her desktop in Los Angeles when my laptop failed me. Thank you to Roger Canaff and Catherine Johnson for answering my investigative questions. Deanna Finn, Izabela Jeremus, and Ashley Previte for beta reading. Charlotte Herscher for her eagle eye. You always make my stories so much better. Mark Klein for being there from the beginning.

A big thanks to Jessica Tribble and Thomas & Mercer for buying this book and continuing to believe in me and my work. I can hardly believe this is already my *fifth thriller* with you!

I am thankful to my beautiful sons, who sacrificed time at the park, several dinners, rides to first grade in the morning, and several weekends without me because I was busy working. You're too young to realize it now, but Mommy actually has a lot more time to spend with you than some other mommies. It's just that my schedule is a little different, so it doesn't always seem that way . . . now.

Finally, I want to thank all my readers. I am so very grateful for each and every one of you. It's because of you that I'm able to write novels for a living. I consider myself extremely fortunate and blessed.

I hope you enjoy this novel.

ABOUT THE AUTHOR

Photo © 2014 Alan Weissman

#1 *USA TODAY* BESTSELLING author Jennifer Jaynes graduated from Old Dominion University with a bachelor's degree in health sciences and a certificate from the Institute for Integrative Nutrition. She made her living as a content manager, webmaster, news publisher, medical assistant, editor, publishing consultant, and copywriter before finally living her dream as a full-time novelist. Jennifer is the author of *The Stranger Inside*, *Never Smile at Strangers*, *Don't Say a Word*, and *Ugly Young Thing*.

When she's not writing or spending time with her husband and twin boys, Jennifer loves reading, cooking, and studying nutrition.

Visit Jennifer at www.jenniferjaynes.net.